VENICE REQUIEM

"Khalid Lyamlahy begins his beautiful and heartbreaking *Venice Requiem* with a dedication: 'In memory of all the Africans who have died far from their homelands, shrouded in silence and oblivion.' Based on the true story of a 22-year-old Gambian refugee who threw himself into Venice's Grand Canal, Lyamlahy revives the countless faceless migrants who lose their lives each year crossing the sea, but also those who experience the terrible loneliness of exile. Thanks to Lyamlahy's reserved and sensitive prose, in an equally graceful translation by Ros Schwartz, we are reminded of our fellow beings all around us and the dangers of erasure."
— Olivia Snaije

This lyrical story of Pateh Sabally, a 22 year old Gambian, who plunged to death in Venice's beautiful Grand Canal, is a many layered look at European morality and culture. Moroccan Khalid Lyamlahy brings Pateh to life through the eyes and emotions of a young french writer who dreams to link Venice and Gambia's Banjul, cities unknown to him, in re-imagining the 5761 kilometre journey of Pateh, his own imagined friend. After his death, looking into the water, the young writer tells Pateh, "Your bequest to Venice: a cracked mirror in which the entire world can see its smugness reflected."
— Victoria Brittain

ALSO BY KHALID LYAMLAHY

Un Roman étranger (Présence Africaine, 2017)
Nostalgic Rebels: Politics, Aesthetics, and Selfhood in Postcolonial Morocco (Liverpool University Press, 2025)

HopeRoad acknowledges the support of le Centre National du Livre (Ministère Français de la Culture) in the translation of this book.

This book is supported by the Institut français (Royaume-Uni) as part of the Burgess programme.

KHALID LYAMLAHY

VENICE REQUIEM

Translated by Ros Schwartz

First published in France
by Présence Africaine, 2023
as *Evocation d'un memorial a Venise*
This translation published in the UK
by Small Axes, an imprint of HopeRoad
17 Kings Avenue
Leeds LS6 1QS

© Khalid Lyamlahy, 2023, 2025
© Présence Africaine, 2023
© Translation, Ros Schwartz, 2025

The right of Khalid Lyamlahy to be identified as the author of this work has been asserted by him, and that of Ros Schwartz to be identied as translator has been asserted by her in accordance with the Copyright, Designs and Patents Act 1988.

All rights reserved. No part of this book may be reproduced, stored in a retrieval system or transmitted in any form or by any means, electronic, mechanical, photocopying, recording or otherwise, without the prior permission of the publishers.

This book is sold subject to the condition that it shall not, by way of trade or otherwise, be lent, re-sold, hired out or otherwise circulated without the publisher's prior consent in any form of binding or cover other than that in which it is published and without a similar condition including this condition being imposed on the subsequent purchaser.

A CIP catalogue record for this book is available from the British Library.

ISBN: 978-1-913109-38-7
e-ISBN: 978-1-913109-47-9

www.hoperoadpublishing.com

This is a work of fiction based on a true event.

In memory of all the Africans who have died far from their homelands, shrouded in silence and oblivion.

" […] there also is the green water of lagoons even drowned I will never be that color to think about you I left all my words at the pawn shop […]"
— Aimé Césaire, *The Miraculous Weapons*

"The Ocean, there at your feet, where those who cannot afford to pay for swimming lessons die . . . swept away, vomiting up and swallowing back down their dreams."
— Mohammed Khaïr-Eddine, *Proximal Morocco*

PART ONE

THE WATERS

I've never seen a man drown. Writing these words already feels unbearable. I don't dare imagine what is to follow. But I have wondered what I would do if I were one day confronted by a drowning man. Would I have the courage to jump into the water to try and save him? The word "courage" would probably not have the same meaning. I tell myself I would at least shout for help, alert passers-by, call the emergency services – in other words, shift any responsibility onto others. A way of confessing my helplessness in the presence of the unspeakable: seeing the spectre of death and instantly admitting defeat.

For the time being, Pateh, you're a news banner running across the bottom of the screen. A dispatch from the *Corriere della Sera* picked up by *Le Monde*, *Le Figaro*, *Le Parisien*, *Ouest-France* and all the local papers. Mindless riffs on the theme of your death. A "tragic death", they call it, as if they needed to reassure themselves and allay any suspicions right away. Categorise your story under the catch-all heading of everyday tragedy.

Pateh, I don't know you, but it's as if your story has taken care of the introductions. An impossible encounter brought about by my naïve need to redeem myself. Once again, I feel as if I'm too late. Like a missed appointment with the blank page. Writing after the fact. Telling myself I needed time to absorb the event or step back from it. All those worn-out excuses proffered so as not to look bad. I'm determined to write, but I already know that no book will suffice to tell the full story, to do justice to your death.

Between Banjul and Venice, your death has exploded into clumps of debris that are impossible to grasp. I write to link the two cities, to create a topography from reports of what happened. To oppose the gaping wound of death with islands of solidarity. Chart your loss, making it oscillate between continent and islands, between bottomless depths and dry land. Reimagine your journey through inevitably fragmented writing.

Faced with the proliferating versions of your story, I must not try to decide between them but instead create a void. Write to free up the tiny space of the funeral oration. Write fast, in one burst, to overcome this feeling of helplessness. Gather up the splinters of a hypothetical portrait, like collecting broken shells on a deserted beach.

It occurs to me that the French word *oraison* (oration) contains both the water that swallowed you (*eau*) and the absence of a reason behind your act (*raison*). The unfathomable reason of the waters that swept you away.

When I decide to write about your death, I know

that I will have to take on Venice. I have never visited that city, but, like everyone else, I've seen countless representations of it. Hosts of images in tourist brochures. Endless photos scrolling on social media. An almost indecent procession of all those supposedly romantic, decadent, legendary places. First self-evident fact: the entire world has visited Venice, but no one has really stopped to consider your death. A world-city enclosing a silent death. A museum-city showing an invisible painting.

On a map of Africa, I put my tentative finger on Gambia. I know little of your mother country. I only know that it's virtually surrounded by Senegal. There is something portentous about this. My gaze follows the River Gambia, a sinuous waterway that plunges inland. The border follows the zigzagging blue line, as if to guide me, the lost reader. The waters slowly close over your name.

You arrive in Venice on Sunday, 22 January 2017. I can feel that insidious cold entering your bones. A cold you've never felt in Italy. Unpleasant shivers run over your skin. A strange feeling of unease. The same questions going round and round. What exactly are you doing here? What are you looking for? Venice whispers that you're not welcome. But who is truly welcome?

From the start, your death brings up images of the thousands of men and women who have drowned in the Mediterranean. I must resist the infinite repetition of your death. Write differently. Rethink writing as an urgent whispering amidst the surrounding din.

I read that in the days before you arrived, it was much colder in Venice. As if the weather had suddenly turned mild. But I had to face facts. The mild weather didn't matter. Variations in temperature would not have changed anything. This was indeed your last winter in the lagoon.

Over the past few days, I've been re-reading Aimé Césaire's *Return to my Native Land*. In my notebook, I copy out this quote: "How much blood is there in my memory. In my memory are lagoons. They are covered with death's heads. They are not covered with water lilies." All those wounds lacerating the body of the continent. I must write to make the waters run dry, to unmask the face of violence, to restore colour to all the waterlilies choked in the silent lagoons.

The newspapers repeat that we know "so little" about you. You're the mystery man of the Grand Canal. A question mark haunting the local and international news. Here and there, bits of your life, scattered, interrupted, like dots on a vast, white canvas.

There are two of you. You and your backpack. The number two, as if thumbing a nose at your solitude. The backpack that was your companion for months.

Silent witness to your departures and arrivals, to your wanderings and your hopes. It was your suitcase, your shopping bag, your makeshift pillow. It was your talisman, your compass. Not a lucky charm, because luck never came into it. Luckiness, a sweet dream fleeing the shores of this high-and mighty, locked, walled-off Europe. A taunting mirage from the banks of the River Gambia.

Yesterday, I came across a short video shot in Zarzis, on Tunisia's south-east coast. The place is called the Cemetery of the Unknown. A man walks among anonymous graves. His name is Shamseddine. Shams – sun in Arabic. A miraculous sun in a grim night. Shamseddine is a fisherman. He speaks of "decomposed bodies", of "half-men and half-women". He pauses, then adds, "with no legs, no head". A moment later, he pours a bottle of water over a small mound. A child's grave, perhaps. He waters some red flowers. Every week, he transports the bodies from the morgue to the cemetery: "If you don't feel the need to do something for these people, you won't do it." The camera films the graves. Heaps of ochre earth spaced barely a few metres apart. On one of them is a notice: "Rose-Marie, Nigeria, 27-5-2017". The only corpse in the cemetery that has been identified. There are four hundred graves in all. Four hundred nails in the world's coffin. Four hundred dead who are waiting, like you, for their funeral oration.

Pozzallo. In my notebook, I write down the name of

the Sicilian town where you landed in 2015. I look it up online. This port town is in the province of Ragusa, in the south-east, around one hundred kilometres from Catania. It's the birthplace of Giorgio La Pira, an academic and prominent figure in Italian Catholicism, who became mayor of Florence in the 1950s and is known for his work promoting interfaith dialogue and bringing together the peoples of the Mediterranean. At the beginning of the twentieth century, Pozzallo was a fishing port before turning into a tourist destination. These days, the town is associated with the regular arrival of refugees. In the shade of the olive trees and fruit trees, stories like yours wash up on the Sicilian shores.

To write is to draw concentric circles around your tragedy. Each word that slips onto the page is a blow to the silence that hangs over your name, to the chasms that open and close to prevent the story from taking shape.

On that 22 January 2017, you arrived in Venice from Milan in the early afternoon. A train journey of some two and a half hours. I looked up the Trenitalia timetable. You must have taken the 12:05 or the 12:35 train. Unless the timetable has changed. You might have been sitting by the window, at the far end of the carriage. Crucial not to attract attention. Sit close to the exit doors. Stay alert and keep your head down. You never know. Things can go wrong, and you must always be prepared for the worst. A lesson from the years of wandering and uncertainty. Your precarious life was always one of escape. The train between Lombardy and Veneto leaves in its wake the irreducible sum of your fears.

My gaze lingers on Pozzallo's beach. A travel agency website extols the charm of the place. The two words used again and again are "relaxation" and "comfort". At one end of the fine-sand beach, a fifteenth-century watchtower now houses a museum. On a map of Sicily, the shoreline looks strangely narrow. I scroll through images as if searching for unexpected signs of your presence here. I close my eyes, and the beach at Pozzallo becomes that long uneven band of overcrowded dinghies, and bodies abandoned to fate.

Four years later, you belong to the archives. Your death is now a file kept in the newspapers' digital memory. The articles about your death are still accessible online. You seem to have become a symbol. I am wary of that word, which reeks of displacement, effacement, hastily and indecently reducing you to an abstraction. A symbol of what, exactly?

I feel I am fighting the inescapable replaying of your death. As if you die again with every word, every image, every scene. I have an insistent craving for a different ending. For a technical glitch, a cancelled train, a journey delayed, your death avoided thanks to some miraculous intervention. Each time, I end up having to accept the facts. The blank page is the mirror of my resignation.

In her book *Au pays des disparus*, the journalist Taina Tervonen attempts to reconstruct the journey of a refugee who died off the coast of Libya in April 2015 after the capsizing of a trawler carrying eight hundred people, all now caged in a wreck lying at a depth of more than three hundred metres. And the question that rises to the surface: how many deaths preceded yours? In my notebook, I copy these words of Taina's: "It was there, in Pozzallo, listening to the stories of all those who dealt with the bodies, that I learned what it means to count the dead."

Perhaps you feel a slight pang as the train pulls out of Milano Centrale station. You think of your first days under the Sicilian sun. You found the streets of Pozzallo extremely narrow. And yet you'd loved those solitary little palm trees in the Piazza delle Rimembranze – the square of memories. Yours had the strange ability to burst out of nowhere like sudden, blinding flashes. Luminous scenes of your home country overlay the fleeting landscapes of this Italy that flashes past the window. Your body is imprinted with the ragged memories of these past two years. The taste of something unfinished that will persist to the end.

The InfoMigrants website reports that on 24 November 2017, almost ten months after your death, a vessel assisted by a fishing boat and carrying two hundred and sixty-four men and women arrived in Pozzallo. Among the group were some forty children and a two-week-old baby. The newborn's mother was nineteen. She fell pregnant after being raped in a Libyan detention camp. I think of that mother cradling the echo of an unpunished crime. She gazes at the horizon which appears close and curved. The low clouds grow more threatening. An eerie silence hangs over the shore. Here, your brothers and sisters are numbers wrapped in foil survival blankets.

Now, Milan belongs to the past. The brutal notion that each stage of your life as an exile will be a nail in your watery coffin. Each train stop pushes you a little closer to the Venetian waters. Brescia, Peschiera, Verona, Vicenza, Padova. Successive stations drum a painful tune in your head. You take refuge in those childhood songs that come back to you like the shattered mirrors of a past life. In the palms of your hands, you believe you can make out a patch of sky over Banjul, a scene from the neighbourhood where you grew up, smiles on your parents' faces, the fragment of a story told by old friends, the ones who didn't have the luck or the heart to leave, the ones who wait for news of their loved ones as if for the late arrival of the new season. Your eyelids, suddenly heavy, close over the remains of a past swallowed up by the tracks.

Misrata, over there, across the sea, is the other face of this tragedy. A thousand and one lives cut short. A thousand and one crimes. A thousand and one graves for a death that does not speak its name. Misrata: the gracious Libyan oasis whose palm trees stand watch over departing coffins.

See Pozzallo again and be reborn. 2015 is the year of all hope. The promise of a new life off the Italian coast. Perhaps you remember the long beach that exhales revenge. Your gaze darts from the few sun umbrellas clustered around the fifteenth-century tower to the slightly faded ones shading the fruit and vegetable stalls of the Albert market in Banjul. Your motherland threads an uncertain path through your memory. Like a venomous snake about to attack, your past hisses, arches back, coils, prides itself on menacing you all the way to this ridiculous seat aboard this train that's sending you slowly toward oblivion.

I hear the screech of the train pulling into Venice station. The window's a border crossing surrounded by barbed wire. Your past life is a ball of wool rolled up in your foreigner's head. All around you, the palpable excitement of all those passengers rushing for the exits. The platform's invaded by yells and laughter, the echoes of which reach you in scattered fragments. Like a cacophonous tune you're unable to make out.

And I feel unspeakable shame at being able to do nothing, or so little, confronted with the procession of those sacrificed lives, of the dead too hurriedly classified, archived, shut out of sight in the opaque drawers of statistics. I write to summon up those faces, emaciated from the cold or exhaustion, the grimaces on chapped lips, the wounds on the maps of bodies and of territories opened but never closed. Pateh, each little scrap of your forgotten story is made from the bitter stuff of shame.

On 15 March 2011, four years before you arrived in Pozzallo, a Moroccan ferry attempted to dock in Sicily to refuel. *Le Monde* reported that Italy denied it access for lack of "certain information" on the passengers. On board the ferry were more than eighteen hundred people evacuated from Libya, where the civil war was at its height. Most of them were Moroccan workers. A *Radio France Internationale* article shows a photo of another ferry arriving in Tangier. Men and women gathered on the deck lean over to inhale the smell of dry land. I'm reminded of an uncle who spent more than fifteen years of his life working on Libyan construction sites. He returned to Morocco in 2000. He told me about a country that no longer exists. He said he knew every street in Tripoli. In the months before he died, he followed events in Libya with a mixture of silent rage and wistful melancholy.

On the concourse of Santa Lucia station, you watch the streams of travellers trailing their suitcases or staring at the departure boards. Some of them look absurd, their faces intent or bewildered. Others display fixed grins. A hundred pairs of eyes glint around your silhouette. A theatre of deformed puppets. The curious feeling you are witnessing an elaborate performance with you as the sole spectator. You are twenty-two years old, and you're bracing yourself to leave this din.

For a long time, I saw writing as a refuge, a release, a place of retreat and regeneration. But I realise that recounting your tragedy is the exact opposite. Taking a huge risk. I may lose all my bearings. It's a parlous attempt to corral a hypothesis, to try to give you back your dignity.

You take your time. Moving away from the platforms without looking back. Walking slowly through the station corridors. Your backpack is even lighter, like a balloon about to fly off. You take your time, putting off entering the world city. You scan the jostling crowds of people in front of the shops or queuing at the vending machines. Avoid the police officers positioned around the station. Despite the constant danger, perhaps you have a novel feeling of detachment. As if, propelled by an invisible hand, you are sliding slowly down a steep slope. As if nothing can hold you back any longer, not even the daylight and the shadows of the buildings that you can already make out on the other side of the Grand Canal.

Images continue to rise to the surface. The waters will spit out their truth in the end. Yesterday, I came across a photo taken in Pozzallo in November 2017, a few months after your death. It shows someone from the Italian Red Cross welcoming a refugee. The man is wrapped in a foil blanket. His head is bowed and in his hands is a folded piece of paper. An official document? A temporary permit? An ID card? The Red Cross representative is wearing blue gloves and a face mask, right hand resting on the refugee's shoulder. The gesture is suspended, as is my gaze, torn between the two figures, like this gulf between us, symbolic of all the gaps, all the failures, all the breaches that end up on the page.

Pateh, this Venice station is the first fragment of a landscape that stubbornly resists the written word. Your tragedy begins here, in this frightening commotion, in the belly of that carefree throng, among those excitable travellers, recognizable by their enormous suitcases or the cameras slung across their shoulders, barely disguising their delight behind the fancy frames of their designer sunglasses or laughing heartily in front of others who look just like them. But who is there to spell out the five letters of your name?

I return obsessively, relentlessly, to the place where you stayed in Sicily. Again, I think about your arrival in Pozzallo, one day in 2015. Did you have those same documents that two years later would be found among your belongings? Did you meet representatives from the Italian Red Cross? Were you too wrapped in a foil survival blanket? I repeat that word, "survival", as if to hold it next to your name a little longer.

I dream of a book that would contain all the words

refused you, all the silences imposed on you. A book where the word "help" is constantly repeated, in which the author would fade from each line, each fragment, to give you back the space denied you in life.

Standing at the top of the stairs in front of Santa Lucia station. Those elongated steps are like the tentacles of a giant octopus. The triple-headed streetlamps spaced a few yards apart cast slender, menacing shadows. The anonymous forms sitting on the steps appear to ignore one another. You look up and your gaze lights on the green copper dome of San Simeone Piccolo, on the other side of the Grand Canal, gleaming in the Sunday afternoon greyness. From afar, the statue of Christ the Redeemer seems to be dancing in the clouds. You are alone. Utterly alone.

How many brothers who left before you drowned in the insatiable whirlpool of the news? How many parents, sisters, mothers, newborns, and couples wrenched from the dawn of uncertain arrivals, forever released from the fear of ID checks, from the yearning for reunions postponed a thousand times? Since when has the rule of the arbitrary been ending lives at the bottom of the sea?

River Gambia, witness to exiles and suffering. Your name rings out from the Fouta Djallon mountain region in Guinea to the Niokolo-Koba National Park in Senegal. Your bitter memory haunts the banks of the Kuluntu, Nieri Ko and Mayél Samu rivers. The waters of your African homeland endlessly hammer out your name. In Banjul, the angry river spills the splinters of your story into the unfeeling, unheeding Atlantic. The belly of the ocean has long since exploded, like a balloon escaped from the realm of childhood.

On the station steps, a semblance of tranquillity. Time stands still, and the Grand Canal looks like a long, bottomless pool. You sit to one side, your backpack wedged between your legs, your hands resting on your knees. You have closed your eyes, but no images have come to disturb you. You're not even hungry. Just a feeling of emptiness inside, as if an invisible hand were slowly undressing you in front of the uncaring city. Quick, open your eyes to shake off this vision. Over there, to the left, the elegant outline of the Ponte degli Scalzi – the Bridge of the Barefoot Monks – like a floating parenthesis, suspended in the air.

In a photo taken in Pozzallo in March 2020, five refugees wait in line behind a metal barrier. Two Italian security guards stand nearby. The five men are wearing identical flip-flops and are gazing in different directions. I focus on the fourth man. His left hand is placed on his chest. In his right, he holds a piece of paper on which I can read what looks like an identification number: 43/C. No surname. No first name. Identity suppressed. How many transparent, flimsy lives are thus abbreviated on scraps of paper?

Behind the words, the mapping of wounds. Yours and those of your brothers and sisters. All those inhospitable territories, hostile plains, lofty mountains, those impractical paths, inaccessible islands, choked estuaries, silted-up roads, and fraught sea crossings – those geographical distances that constantly reflect ruptures, gashes, breaks. I write as if reading an ancient, creased map of the world. All I see are broken lines, blurred shapes, approximate geometries, encircled spaces that become disrupted and dizzying. Before my eyes, the hemispheres merge, continents change places, borders dissolve, waters have the pale colour of defeat. Like an immense expanse of mud abruptly closing over your memory.

Waiting. Those long, interminable minutes on the steps of Santa Lucia station. Who knows, maybe someone will come and talk to you, ask you the time, inquire about train departures or the quickest route to the Rialto Bridge. Maybe you'll slip on your backpack again and turn around. Take the train back to Milan and find a way to get to Sicily. Maybe you'll even reach Pozzallo with its comforting palm trees, quiet, narrow streets and beach of fine sand. You'll think about going home finally. In Banjul, you'll tell them it didn't work out, your journey ended on the steps of an Italian railway station, your dream fell into the Grand Canal, soundlessly, without a ripple, like a pebble in a puddle of water. But there are too many maybes. Too many what-ifs. A howling lack of certainty in the face of the inevitable.

I have a constant need to reflect on the gap between writing your story and that of Venice. As if a secret had crept into the chasm and now it had to be revealed. I picture the green copper dome of San Simeone Piccolo. It will mirror your fragility, be the silent witness to your death.

Groping as I write. Stumbling narrative. Stuttering memory. Sentences tailing off. How can I recount your death other than in the broken thread of a text to come? I feel I must write in the margin of your death, push words along a ridge, string together images up to the brink of the precipice.

I found two photos of you online. In the first, you're wearing a blue, patterned shirt. In the second, a black jacket with a stiff collar. With your left hand, you're making a slanting V-sign. A victory that needs straightening up. A victory that smacks of defeat.

The ballet of the ACTV logos on the hulls of the water buses. Your serene gaze follows the forest of hands loading and unloading suitcases, trying to calm excited children or handle bags that are nothing like yours. A few yards to the left, you see the vaporetto stop with its yellow bands and the word Ferrovia. People are queuing on the ramp. For the time being, you have no desire to move. Your bag is still wedged between your knees, like a final link to your past life.

My gaze constantly flits between Pozzallo and Venice on the map. It occurs to me that your story is surrounded by water. The Ionian Sea. The Adriatic Sea. The Tyrrhenian Sea. Water delineates a vast geography of loss whose echoes resonate as far as the banks of River Gambia. Your homeland carries water in its belly foreshadowing those neighbouring seas flowing into one another and suspended on the borders of Europe.

I recall a memory from Oued Laou, a coastal town in northern Morocco. Some forty kilometres from Tetouan, the gentle whiff of summer holidays. On Saturdays, at the village market, the traditional headdresses glitter in the sun. On a clear day, Spain is visible from the shady balcony. The beach stretches to infinity and the horizon continuously recedes. At night, shadows push a flimsy boat along the beach. In the distance, whispers. Wan torch beams. Shapes moving around. The thrumming of an engine starting up. A light that's extinguished in the sea. Each boat that leaves makes me think of you. That was at the end of the last century, but it feels as if it were yesterday. Pateh, I saw with my own eyes men from my country head into the night and vanish.

Writing in brief snatches to ease the burden of the story. The only writing possible is that which leaves an imprint.

A sudden, unexpected flash of sunlight on the surface of the water. It's time to stand up and walk away from those dreary steps and face the city. On the opposite bank of the Grand Canal, the houses now look like cardboard boxes whose windows are dark, menacing little holes. Again, that feeling of malign cold that seeps into your pores. You slide a hand inside a pocket to check the plastic wallet.

To the south of the Sicily that welcomed you one day in 2015, an archipelago of names makes me giddy. I look for traces of your passage on those tiny islands scattered between the territorial waters of Tunisia and Italy. Off the coast of Sfax, the Tunisian Kerkennah Islands stare at their Italian counterparts of Lampedusa and Linosa. A little further north, it's only seventy kilometres between the Italian island of Pantelleria and Cape Bon, the north-eastern tip of Tunisia. Curious symmetry between these unsuspected geographical proximities. Fascinating distribution of these island fragments that have broken away from the imposing continental land masses.

In my notebook, I jot down this description of Venice by Goldoni: "Maps, plans, models and descriptions are insufficient; it must be seen. All other cities bear more or less resemblance to one another, but Venice resembles none." I wonder whether Venice's unique character has something to do with your decision, Pateh. A final halt to be done with maps, plans and descriptions. Your presence alone in Venice speaks louder than any words or interpretations.

From my reading, I learn that you have a cousin who also lives in Italy. His name is Muhammed. Apparently, you haven't met up since your arrival in the country, even though your families are from the same village, Wellingara, and know each other. I look it up on the map. The village is in the Kombo North district, some twenty kilometres southwest of Banjul. There's very little information online about Wellingara. One article reports that in 2013, two years before you left, a new mosque was inaugurated in the presence of around a hundred people, including from the neighbouring villages. What were you doing in 2013? Were you already thinking of leaving?

You walk beside the Grand Canal. Your first few steps warm you up. Perhaps you pause under a streetlamp to watch one last time the comings and goings of the vaporetti and the tourists milling around. Some take selfies with the dome of San Simeone Piccolo in the background. They twist and turn to get the best shot. Others, much more discreet, stand glued to the spot, as if mesmerised by the alluring body of the city slowly spreading out before their eyes. A few yards further on, level with Calle Carmelitani, opposite the Ferrovia stop, you get your first glimpse of the gondolas lined up between the wooden posts. Their slender, dark shapes look like long coffins floating on the water.

All those dreams of dignity reduced to dust. All those hopes and dreams crushed under the weight of indifference. All those plans put on hold or nipped in the bud. What is left after so much heartbreak if not the desire to escape, to slam the door, to seek refuge in the silent detonation of death?

And this perpetual question eats away at me: Why Venice? To scream your pain to the world or to leave a bubble of silence amid the tumult? You could have stayed in Milan or tried your luck in another town in northern or central Italy. Waited for a break, for better days, the chance to start all over again elsewhere. Repeating over and over that "the best is to come", that "nothing is ever completely lost", that two years is a relatively short time, that you must remain strong. You could have. The searing pain of that "could have", as if writing were forever doomed to be a resurgence of regrets.

Some articles suggest that in Pozzallo you'd been given a residence permit "on humanitarian grounds". Others add that it had been revoked, which would have affected you very badly. The residence permit: that triumph of the temporary and the conditional, that ingenious way of making human beings suffer the vagaries of bureaucracy, the fluctuation of political moods, the strange formality of paperwork assembled in a state of anxiety and uncertainty, the absurd accumulation of two or three copies of documentary evidence, documents signed, stamped and certified, official requests lodged on appointments made months in advance, interrogations by cynical agents in gloomy offices, long queues exuding fear and humiliation, waiting weeks and months to obtain a piece of paper, a laminated card, a proof of life or of survival, immediately threatened by the worry that it is about to expire.

How many foreigners before you have set foot in this city with a backpack and dreams on hold? As you gaze at the Grand Canal, you dimly recall the blurred faces of those brothers you glimpsed in the stations of Brescia, Verona or Padova. They were on the platforms, leaning against a pillar or slumped on the steps. They had a sad weariness about them, their spirits visibly tormented by the relentless brief halts and new departures, by the frenetic pace of long journeys and dead-end transfers. You think back to those left behind at the Pozzallo reception centre, those sent off to accommodation facilities in Sicily, those waiting for a decision or an appeal. You need to free your gaze, but from your vantage point, the horizon is obscured by the Bridge of the Barefoot Monks. You know that you are going to have to confront that bridge and gradually get used to the intimidating shadow of its arch.

In a photo taken in Wellingara, children are kicking a ball on a makeshift football ground. One of them is watching the game from a distance, arms akimbo, affecting indifference. The goalposts are two long sticks driven into the ground. In another photo, taken in front of a school entrance, children cluster in front of the camera. They're all dressed in lemon-yellow tops and purple bottoms. I look for your features in the radiant smiles of those Gambian children. At the end of the 90s, you were among them. I wonder whether you were already dreaming of other skies.

I'd dreamed of Venice for a long time from reading writers who had visited the city or had lived there. Now that your story haunts me, I need to return to those writings, as if to seek answers there, clues, keys that would help me come to terms with the void left by your death, the inexplicable act, the signs of the tragedy to come. Over the past few days, the names of the Venetian palaces have been going round and round in my head: Ca' d'Oro, Vendramin, Grimani, Palazzo Grassi, Ca' Rezzonico, Ca' Foscari, Ca' Pesaro, Palazzo Fortuny. Mellifluous, outdated names, like vestiges of a bygone era. In my notebook, I write down this quotation by Michel Tournier: "You watch the dramatic façades of the palaces go past, each with their private landing stage and the posts painted with multicoloured spirals where the gondolas are moored, like nervous horses, but you constantly look down at the heavy, turbulent swell, churned up by the oars and the propellers, like a black milk." My head suddenly heavy, I think I can hear the painful lament of the gondolas as each oar stroke plunges your story a little deeper in the fathomless depths of the waters.

In late September 2019, seventy North Africans landed on the island of Pantelleria, to the south of Sicily. At first, the smugglers took them on board large fishing boats, then, when they reached the limits of Italian territorial waters, transferred them onto small boats. Here are these brothers, tossed about, manhandled, thrown from one point to another like cases of freight on a cargo route. One day, someone should write about all those arrivals that are similar to yours, collect together those experiences shaped by the law of human trafficking, oppose to the disconcerting precision of statistics the beating of frightened hearts in leaky tubs cravenly left to the mercy of the waves. One day, someone should lift up the surface of the water and spell out the names of all the drowned.

In front of Santa Maria di Nazareth, opposite the water taxi stop, you pause for perhaps a few seconds. There is something intimidating about the imposing door of the seventeenth-century church, also known as the Church of the Scalzi (Church of the Barefoot). The twin columns are like tree trunks reaching for the sky. There is something soothing, almost unreal, about the white marble. The statues of saints in the alcoves appear to be staring directly at you with their vacant, lifeless eyes. Once again, the oppressive solitude causes a knot to form in your stomach and your throat to tighten. All about you, the world continues to go round as if you had never existed.

Contrary to the guidebooks is the perverse idea that this city is an immense sleeping cemetery, that the waters of the Grand Canal will eventually dry up to reveal hitherto invisible coffins, carefully concealed from the gaze of the millions of tourists who visit the city each year. A nightmare vision that haunts me, with the five letters of your name recurring like a terrible, persistent refrain.

For the past few days, I've been taking an interest in the island of Pantelleria, off the Tunisian coast. In June 1943, the Allies invaded it to take advantage of its strategic position to facilitate their landing in Sicily. One month later, during the Sicilian campaign, they relied on the help of the Moroccan and Algerian Goumiers – indigenous soldiers – to tackle the island's steep mountains. Their capture of Mounts Campanito, Coniglio and Acuto has gone down in the annals of history. Those events feel surprisingly close. Nowadays, the too rapidly forgotten exploits of the Algerian infantry divisions and the Moroccan Tabor units resonate with the arrival of their compatriots aboard makeshift boats. Pateh, time passes, but our landings still have the same bitter taste, that of fleeting, conditional, suspect victories, of which there will soon be nothing but a few lines in a dusty history textbook.

That sweet illusion when writing believes itself capable of connecting fragments separated by miles of borders or years of silence. To write about your story, I have to take account of the limitations of writing, recognise the part that is lacking, incomplete, the gaps in each fragment.

As you turn around, your gaze meets that of the vendor who has one of the little stalls facing the Church of the Scalzi. His piercing eyes look you up and down with a mixture of distrust and pity. Three elderly women, obviously tourists, stop at his stall and start trying on straw hats and sunglasses. Pulling faces, they come and go in front of a long mirror that's slightly damaged on one side. The vendor does his utmost to persuade them, all the while keeping an eye on you. Your heart and the residence permit in your pocket have never felt so heavy.

The universal story still waiting to be written is that of all those passing through, shunted about, wrenched from their lands, packed into nameless boats, lined up behind barbed-wire fences or on gangways, transferred from one border to the next, unwanted like on the first day, extradited on special flights, crushed in the anonymity of stations and transit areas. A universal story to show that you are neither an exception nor a tragedy. Just the mirror of a collective wound that the world obstinately refuses to dress.

This city's past is like a shadow stalking the story. On admiring a painting by Canaletto, I indulge in the strange pursuit of looking for signs of life and death in eighteenth-century Venice. I easily recognise the columns of the Church of the Scalzi and the dome of San Simeone Piccolo, which has just been built. I can see a woman hidden in the cabin of a gondola and the hazy forms of small groups strolling along the quays. The houses beyond the Church of the Scalzi would be knocked down around the mid nineteenth century to make way for the railway station. I follow the gondolas that fan out like fine ink stains in the pale waters. My gaze lingers on those gondoliers with alarming dark faces, ferrymen of those invisible hells that haunt human memory. Your death hounds me even into the obsolete perspective of the Venetian painter.

From the start, I have resisted the urge to return to Thoman Mann's novel. Avoid the easy shortcut. Refrain from associations that would reduce your story to an object or to a literary fantasy. All the same, there is something captivating about Mann's descriptions, like the gondola that Aschenbach boards: "The strange craft, an entirely unaltered survival from the times of balladry, with that peculiar blackness which is found elsewhere only in coffins – it suggests silent, criminal adventures in the rippling night, it suggests even more strongly death itself, the bier and the mournful funeral, and the last silent journey." I close the book, but the lapping of the waters continues to resonate in my head. A series of short, sharp sounds interspersed with worrying silences. That night, I have a disturbing dream. A hundred or so biers swirl on the surface of the canal in a compelling ceremony. Then, all of a sudden, your face emerges from the waters. I recognise you. You look as if you're trying to shout, but no sound comes from your mouth. The next moment, your face disintegrates and you disappear, leaving a trail of dust.

And you reappear in front of my eyes of the anxious scribe. I'm unable to say whether you are still in the same place in front of the imposing door of the Scalzi facing the vendor of hats and sunglasses or whether you've taken a few steps towards the bridge. I can see only your backpack swaying from right to left like a beacon shining in an overcast sky. Santa Lucia station is now a forbidding mass lying beneath the clouds. Milan and Pozzallo have never been so far away.

I have this compulsion to dwell on the images and to speculate on the meaning of your departure, on the things that you took with you and those you gave to your loved ones. I pause at a photo of a kindergarten class taken in Wellingara. I count eight tables. Four children per table. The ones who couldn't find a chair are standing, spread around the room. On the back wall is the alphabet in large letters. The side walls with flaking paint are covered in children's drawings. The shutters of the wide, vertical windows are half open. My attention is drawn to the little satchels lined up on the windowsills. I immediately think of your backpack. How many of those satchels will remain on the windowsills waiting for better times? How many of those children will leave school and make the perilous journey north?

Now and again, I am struck by the obstinate thought that Venice is a slimy octopus that puts out its tentacles to grab your memory and crush your chest where a thousand vessels beat, ferrying your story to other islands, other archipelagos, other pieces of land scattered a long way from your native country. The French alchemist Limojon de Saint-Didier, who died in a shipwreck in 1689, compared Venice's Grand Canal to a "huge vein that maintains and refreshes all the tiniest parts of this city's vast body through its many little tributaries". And what if the huge vein were to explode around your name? What would remain of your battle with the city other than the silence of the lagoon and the indolence of the world?

This writing is condemned to the to-ing and fro-ing, to the endless wandering between the river of your home country and the canals of the country of others. It is a writing of oscillation and vertigo. And yet, I know I have to tame the words, hold them in respect, push them to the borders of fiction while keeping them in the tentative domain of restitution.

You stand rooted to the spot in front of the first sandwich bar with a green awning. You aren't hungry. You have no money. You have nothing to bequeath, nothing to think, nothing to say to this city that exudes wealth and defeat. You look up and your gaze rests on the seven shutters with rusty paintwork. All closed. Seven shutters like the seven gates of a nameless hell. You have a sudden urge to rap on the seven windows and then run away. Don't hesitate. Seven sharp raps to shake up this slumbering continent. Seven sharp raps to illuminate the dark face or the world. Rap seven times then run until you are out of breath. Don't turn around. Don't stop. All along the Grand Canal those seven raps echo like a final warning before the crash.

And so it will be the solitude of the outsider against the vertiginous number of bridges. This city has nearly four hundred, built of stone, brick or iron. They stand there, aligned on the map, suspended like all those questions without answers that dog your journey. You won't have the time to see them, but they will ensure that snippets of your tragedy are spread. Your lagoonal solitude amplified by the city's architectural unity.

The island geography has this fascinating ability to trace a historical continuum, to reverse-shape stories whose echoes reverberate from one island to another, like a vast palace with countless rooms. I see battalions of African forebears telling other stories of painful departures, other wounds suffered in the prime of life, other tragedies caused by the violence of being wrenched away and then of oblivion. Pateh, your story plucks the chords of an aching memory. Here I am in June 1944, when the Senegalese infantrymen and the Moroccan Goumiers were preparing to take the fighting to the Island of Elba. In a photo snapped on Corsica as they boarded a barge, my gaze is drawn to a poor overloaded mule at the foot of a gangway. A Goumier is trying to push him forward under the eye of the watching French soldiers. I look at this mule as I think about my own writing which is battling decades of mute suffering and pernicious amnesia. In the stifled memory of your forebears, I see hazy reflections of your story.

Not surprisingly, the Venice lagoon projects its fragility onto the text. *Acqua alta* is the name of a threat that grows worse with the years. I skim through alarming articles that are a reminder of the rising sea levels in Venice, the sinking of the city, the subsidence of the ground, the erosion of the lagoon. I read everywhere that Venice is under the threat of inevitable disappearance. Your story is intertwined with that of the dying city. A strange coincidence that no one foresaw. Ideas for saving the city abound: finalise the plan to build barriers, pump water into the subsoil, install hydraulic pumps, regulate mass tourism. To salvage what is left of your memory, there are few words; the silences are long and heavy. It is easy to sense an unavowed, persistent, insurmountable difficulty.

Perhaps you are pacing up and down in front of the sandwich bar. You count the clouds on the city's rooftops. You watch the people – their hands, bodies, wiggling hips, calls, smiles, footsteps – while the imperceptible movements of the water that awaits you, taunts you, sends a signal that you alone pick up and decode. Perhaps you empty your mind. You expel the memories of the crossing and your arrival. You close your eyes and open them again at once to shut out the smugglers' threats, to stifle your brothers' cries of distress and dispel the image of trembling lips, wan eyes, pale faces, fingers linked in the dark, fitful breathing, jerky movements, the pitiful gasping of an Africa dying far from its shores.

The lexicon of Venice contains a strange opposition between the living and the evanescent. I discover the fascinating concepts of dead lagoon and living lagoon. The areas where the tide can be felt form the living lagoon, which also corresponds to the part that's closest to the shore. The other areas make up the so-called dead lagoon – or less living – crisscrossed with marshes, lakes and canals. Around the middle of the seventeenth century, an investigation by the Magistrato alle Acque – the institution in charge of managing the lagoon – became interested in separating the living lagoon from the dead lagoon. The history of the lagoon is written between the ambition to develop shipping and the need to safeguard the land area. The waters or dry land: that fatal dilemma where your tragedy lands.

In January 2019, almost two years after your death, The Gambia and Senegal inaugurated the Senegambia Bridge. The bridge spans the river from the Gambian town of Farafenni and helps connect north and south Senegal. Until then, the only way across the river for people and vehicles was by ferry. The term most frequently used in the press is 'opening up'. Opening up in the sense of ending the isolation of the Casamance region and improving communications between the two countries. Reading the newspaper reports, I realise that I am writing to open up your story, to attach it to the world and build a bridge of words and images between the emptiness of your loss and the surfeit of information.

As I continue to think about the concepts of living lagoon and dead lagoon, Venice's topography breaks up into concentric circles that close in on each fragment of your tragedy. My writing is in a way besieged by the city. The words that wash up on the page are trapped between the pincers of the lagoon. During the course of my reading, I come across these words by the poet Marc Alyn: "Between the living lagoon and the dead lagoon are strung the islands, each one forming a closed world". It is the sum of those closed worlds that constitutes the fragmented and unfathomable space of your tragedy.

You stare fixedly at the stall crammed with souvenirs opposite the sandwich bar. Hats, bags, bracelets, necklaces, postcards, ornamental plates, trays decorated with the emblems of the city, kitchen utensils, T-shirts and all sorts of gadgets. The word "Venezia" is repeated on all of them, like a refrain on a loop. Every boat that stops at Ferrovia sets off again with a piece of the city and a fragment of those fleeting moments prior to your final act.

On the night of Friday 3 August 2018, two sixty-nine-year-old fishermen are on a boat at the Lido San Nicolò canal stop at the mouth of the Venice lagoon. At around midnight, a craft with four youths on board rams the fishermen's boat. The first fisherman dies on the way to hospital, and the second is retrieved after two hours. The two men were "lifelong friends" according to *Le Dauphiné*. For some days, I've been haunted by the image of those two men chatting on board their boat shortly before the accident. What could they have been talking about? Old memories of their Venetian youth or tales of marvellous fish gleaming in the nets? About the composition of the latest Italian government or the gradual decline of fishing in the lagoon? Had they, a year earlier, heard about you? So many questions swallowed up by those same waters that they had plied for so long. Dead the same day, a few minutes apart, taking with them the memory of their friendship and a few murmurs in the Venice night.

You, the young African, the exile from Gambia, the refugee from Pozzallo, the lone traveller from Milan, the man with the backpack arriving in Venice: now you are alone in front of the greenish waters of the lagoon. A solitary figure feeling removed, separated, eradicated.

I go back to Canaletto's paintings as if only art can help me fill the vacuum surrounding your death. For the first time, I am struck by the animated scenes depicted. Men conversing beneath the colonnades of St Mark's Square close to the Caffè Florian, dignitaries and ambassadors leaving the Church of San Rocco after the Solemn Mass celebrating the eponymous saint, gondolas clustered on Ascension Day for the Marriage of the Sea ceremony, vendors and other onlookers chatting in small groups along the Riva degli Schiavoni promenade near the Doge's Palace. Every scene is teeming with unfinished details, untold stories, commemorations taking place by the water with superimposed images of departures and arrivals in a dizzying whirl. Each scene revives the question: why Venice? At this point, I am not seeking an answer anymore. It is enough for me to have understood that you slowly blended into the legendary hubbub of this city. It will no longer be only the Venice of Canaletto, but also the Venice where Pateh died one afternoon in January 2017.

In front of the souvenir stall, nothing has moved. Contemplating the vertical columns of postcards, I wonder who you might have written to had you had the time or the inclination. To your cousin in Milan? To your parents? To an elderly uncle in Wellingara? To a friend from Pozzallo? Or simply to your entire family? You might have chosen a postcard with gondolas swaying beneath a bridge, or palaces lit up at night. Or maybe a picture of St Mark's campanile, a stone's throw from the famous basilica, like a finger pointing skywards. You might have sat on the steps of the Church of the Scalzi to scribble a few words then you'd have carefully stuck on the stamp before sliding the card into the red letterbox you'd noticed near the sandwich bar. And it's as if the whole world could have received your card, interpreted your words, read your testament before consigning you to the infallible machine of oblivion.

My reading around the subject of your home country takes me to the uninhabited island of Kunta Kinteh, formerly James Island, at the mouth of the River Gambia. Listed as a UNESCO World Heritage Site in 2003, the island was a hub of the slave trade and colonisation. In 2011, the island was renamed Kunta Kinteh after the famous Gambian rebel slave who was captured and transported to Annapolis, in Maryland. In 1976, the American writer Alex Haley paid tribute to him in his novel *Roots*. Photos of the island show the little landing stage and the ruined buildings of former British colonial administration offices, flanked by rusty cannons encircled by a few scattered baobabs. Among the ruins are the remains of the prisons where the slaves were locked up. I learn that the island is shrinking due to the continual erosion. A CNN article even writes of "the fight to save Kunta Kinteh". My gaze lingers on the scrawny, thinning baobabs, stubborn witnesses to a memory that refuses to fade. I close my eyes and I see those same baobabs transposed to the banks of the Grand Canal, alongside the lampposts in front of Santa Lucia station to create a forest of silhouettes ready to reach out and hold you back.

As I write, I keep coming back to the irreconcilable tension between life and death in Venice. It's as if everything in this submerged city were an invitation to cross the porous frontier between the here and elsewhere, to slide slowly along a dangerous ridge stretching endlessly and changing direction. As if the dead and the living were forever linked to the sinuous course of the waters, ready to engulf them or to spew them out. I copy out these words by Philippe Sollers: "The dead support Venice from afar, they are in transit; like the living, they float, like them, in a parenthesis on the surface". I don't want to see you "in transit", or in the news banners or on the blank page. I'm struggling against the prospect of losing you again while the world is busy perfecting its noisy, chaotic dance at the water's edge.

I think of your home country and rewrite these pages by reversing the sense of history, by gluing together the fragments as best I can. I shan't erase the gaps but will reinsert them into the hollows of your journey. All the articles about your tragedy insist on keeping you a prisoner of Venice, as if your life before didn't count, as if your family didn't exist, as if your past no longer mattered and that the only way of paying homage to you had to start with Venice. How do I escape such a bind?

Above the wooden door between the two sandwich bars, you spot an eighth shutter that's half open. A shadow appears to be moving behind the curtains. Unless it's my imagination again that keeps inventing anonymous witnesses to your solitude. The tourists who walk past you cross the Bridge of the Barefoot Monks, picking up their colourful suitcases or continuing straight along Rio Terà Lista de Spagna. To your left, others dive straight into the Hotel Bellini, its ochre façade and stone balconies recognisable from a distance.

I wonder whether you gaze after them or whether you simply watch their silhouettes vanish into the crowd. The hotel is located in an eighteenth-century palace and it's as if the burdensome history of this city were again smothering the narrative.

La Serenissima unsettled by your tragedy. I wonder whether the city's honorary title will still mean anything after this 22 January 2017. How is it possible to find an ounce of serenity after the terrible detonation of your death?

Opposite the island of Kunta Kinteh, on the north shore of River Gambia, the map shows the village of Albreda, a former French trading post which for a long time was a slave market. A statue represents a former slave whose head is in the form of a globe. Freed from their chains, his arms are raised to the sky to embrace his new-found freedom. On his chest, the symbol of the Kanga mask reminds me of the logo of the magazine, *Présence Africaine*. At his feet, on the base of the statue, is this slogan that sums up humanity's wish in the face of the abominable: "Never again!"

It is reported that you walked along the Grand Canal "for a few minutes". A terse formula to sum up those long moments when we know nothing of your thoughts, your emotions, your frame of mind. Your story is already beyond our grasp. Free and elusive.

In the tourist brochures, your native Gambia is celebrated as "the smiling coast of Africa". The publicity boasts of the friendly welcome and the locals' unwavering smiles, the warm sun bathing the white sand beaches, the swaying coconut palms on the horizon, the procession of cows savouring the afternoon calm, the delicious cuisine consisting of benachin, domoda or yassa, the profusion of sights and colours at Serrekunda Market on Sayerr-Jobe Avenue or at the craft market along the Senegambia Road. Each year, 150,000 tourists visit your country. Some, it seems, come for a taste of the "authentic African experience and privileged contact" with the locals.

Leave Italy? Did you think of doing so? You could have crossed the border into France and perhaps continued northwards. Many try their luck on the other side of the Alps. They follow the trails in small groups, trudging for more than five hours over steep mountain passes and facing the bitter cold with their unsuitable clothing and makeshift gear. Some reach Montgenèvre, others Briançon, less than fifteen kilometres from the Italian frontier. In an article from February 2019, I read that a group had to carry the body of one of their number who had frozen to death. He had neither hat nor gloves.

I close my eyes and dream of crossing River Gambia to soak up the lights and colours of your homeland. I picture the mangrove forests with luminous mossy roots, the farms where the mountains of oysters glint in the sunlight like diamonds, the peaceful villages where people cultivate rice and groundnuts, where majestic kapok trees grow, their slender trunks and heavy, spreading crowns reaching skywards like giant figurines. I see your homeland in the vibrant murmur of its ecosystems; I soak up the beauty of this enthralling nature, pulsating with stories and well-kept secrets. Each boat that sails up the river will bring me a little closer to your silent truths.

Facing the Bridge of the Barefoot Monks, you follow the delicate undulations of the waters for the last time. Perhaps the shimmering reflections of the light appear more aggressive. The clouds gather a little more densely over the uneven rooftops. The people now look like wax dolls moving slowly down a long, static platform. Santa Lucia station sleeps above its empty flights of steps. The Church of the Scalzi is no more than a giant shadow whose pillars look slender and incomplete. The shutters above the sandwich bars are opaque rectangles in the middle of a peeling surface. In your suddenly light head, Venice is a heap of ruins about to slide into the Grand Canal.

In the silence that precedes the great nothingness, the aisles of the Banjul craft market form a dazzling rainbow which I try to contrast with the Venetian gloom. I conjure up brightly coloured bags and necklaces, dresses with dancing patterns, piles of wicker baskets, joyful sheets decorated with elephants and crocodiles, wax print fabrics on invisible hangers, wooden carvings lined up on the ground as in a festival with no music, processions of figures surrounded by silent drums. I slip into the skin of a scribe wandering through those bustling streets. In my notebook, I write that every inch of this country remembers your name.

Following the broken line of palaces and mansions along the banks of the Grand Canal, my gaze lingers on the altane, those strange terraces set on the rooftops. I look at the wooden structures overlooking the lagoon, watching the activity on the quaysides and the gliding gondolas, the way one watches from an attic window the signs of life going on, impassive, impervious, imperturbable. Maybe you too dreamed of a window looking out onto the realm of childhood, onto a last summer on the banks of River Gambia, among the youths lolling against the pirogues and gazing at the horizon.

5761 kilometres. That's the distance between Banjul and Venice. More than one hundred times the size of the lagoon. Each kilometre is a gash in the body of the foreigner, a scar on his face, a notch in his interrupted life story.

A dozen or so seconds looking at your ID document through the waterproof wallet. The layer of plastic like a border between the urgency of the present and the gulfs of the past. The sudden compulsion to wipe everything out. Withdraw from the world and its hubbub. Your actions are precise. As you set your bag down near the Bridge of the Barefoot Monks, your hand is steady.

At low tide, when your smile is already fading, in front of my eyes appear the images of those women setting out to harvest oysters in the mangroves of River Gambia. The slender shapes of their pirogues glide slowly along the creeks. I see them rowing, bare hands and feet, their gaze fixed on the far end of the bolongs, their songs echoing between the two shores. A little later, their hands are busy pulling off the oysters attached to the roots of the mangrove trees. The strokes of the machete or the axe, their palms gripping the forked sticks, their feet sunk in the poto-poto, their pagnes hitched up to their knees, the plaited baskets lined up in the bottoms of the pirogues. As they weave in and out of the mangrove forest, the dignity of those women is like a scarlet glow lighting up your exile's face.

My reading about Venice introduces me to a vocabulary where water constantly sculpts the language. Islands and canals intertwined, chaotic, dizzying archipelagos, tight, sandy strips, crossing points disappearing and reappearing on the map, natural and artificial channels embedded in the lagoon, surfaces prey to the power of the waters, subject to the natural laws of submersion and erosion. Here, writing is more than a crossing. It is a continuous negotiation with this evasive, unstable aquatic lexicon, tormenting both landscapes and language.

Your bag is now set down close to the bridge. The train ticket and residence permit are still in the plastic wallet. A timid dying ray strikes your forehead. If I blink, I can see a hundred Gambian children running on the beach, slipping between the colourful pirogues, stopping every so often to point at the receding horizon. The memory of a country and of a continent beating in your breast. The articles I look up are categorical: it is around 3.30 pm when you throw yourself into the water of the Grand Canal.

PART TWO

THE SCREAMS

I don't recall the exact moment when I made the decision to go to Venice. All I know is that I did everything I could to put off that moment. As if I were afraid of once again facing up to your death, to the incomprehension at the scene of the tragedy. I think I was afraid too of finding myself inadvertently in the role of the journalist or the investigator. I am neither. I write with the dignity of the defeated. I am not trying to win a battle or to re-establish a truth. Only to plough a furrow in the chilling memory of your death.

Eyewitnesses reported that you didn't waver when you threw yourself into the water. It was a clean, rapid, almost instantaneous jump. Around you, stunned looks and the panorama of the apathetic, sleepy city gently preparing for the coming spectacle.

I read that in the early 1990s, Venice took in numerous refugees fleeing the war in the former Yugoslavia. The municipal authorities set up reception centres and support services. Venice was hailed as a City of Refuge in reference to a network supported by the International Parliament of Writers whose members include Jacques Derrida, Édouard Glissant and Toni Morrison. Refuge:

"To provide a refuge, shelter, or retreat for (a person); to shelter, protect." (Oxford English Dictionary), or "To seek or take refuge; to seek shelter or protection." It may have been no coincidence that you chose Venice. Flee the difficulties that had dogged you since your arrival in Italy. Seek help, a refuge, support. Even if it meant doing so in such a dramatic way.

Packing my bag for Venice, I include my notebook and the file I've put together over the past few weeks. Press cuttings, copies of articles, photos, notes taken from my reading, pencil diagrams. I know I'll need time to study the materials gathered since the start of my research. Most importantly, I don't want to re-read my notes during the trip. I want to be open to all the fragments to come and to be alert to the echoes of your story as they continue to come together.

No matter how hard I close my eyes and try to visualise the exact moment when you threw yourself into the Grand Canal, no image appears. I realise that to carry on writing, I have to rely on a precarious collection of uncorroborated eyewitness accounts, vague and dubious descriptions. Apparently, there's a video. For the time being, I don't want to watch it. I'm not ready to face the horror.

In the past few days, I've been reminded of an online video. On Bijilo beach, some ten kilometres from Banjul, young Gambians in their twenties are playing an improvised football match. Their joyful shouts are partially drowned out by the crashing of the waves. I can't make out their faces. Do they know those children I saw previously in a classroom? Will they leave the country like you to follow the arduous routes north? Will they end up in the hands of unscrupulous people-smugglers? Who will take the trouble, when dusk falls, to spell out their names on the empty beach?

On the eve of my departure, my backpack is ready. My flight and hotel in Venice are booked. I decide to get back to work, but I can't. Sitting at my desk, I have a sudden urge to shout. To close my eyes and hear myself shout. Forget the words, the city, the waters, the gondolas, the water-taxis, the postcards, the figures on the station steps, the tourists' dumbfounded expressions, the stalls lining the quaysides, the newspaper headlines, the news tickers, the hotels' sombre façades, the outpourings of tributes and indignation, the flashbulbs, the imposing bulks of the churches, the cold surface of the marble, the formulaic articles, the bridges' dancing arches, the fleeting romances beneath the lights of the palaces, the potential failure of a narrative that risks losing you amid a tide of useless words. Shout to give myself a moment of respite before the thunderous return of the silence.

Apparently, the Grand Canal is particularly cold at the spot where you jumped in. No warmer than five degrees Celsius. The water is deep, bottomless, unfathomable. Like a vast freezing basin whose bed cannot be seen.

Weave other stories around yours. Expand the canvas of the story to make a procession of perfectly visible lives. On the InfoMigrants website I read that on the morning of 23 May 2021, in a Turin detention centre, Musa, a twenty-three-year-old Guinean, was found hanged in a noose made from his bedsheets. Two weeks earlier, he'd been beaten up in the streets of Ventimiglia. Despite a stay in hospital, the young man was still weak and depressed, coldly abandoned to his vulnerability. From the isolation cell where he'd been placed, he had cried out countless times, called for help, asked for a doctor. No response. The pristine sheet was his last resort.

At the Orly bus stop, I put away the newspaper bought from the kiosk on Place Denfert-Rochereau and lean against the glass wall. I overhear snatches of conversation. Young compatriots of mine, probably students, are on their way to Morocco. I recognise the excitement of returning home. An unlikely mix of apprehension and joy. The faces of our loved ones that we imagine on the bus windows. The emotion of being reunited that we experience ten times in our heads. The first words that we mutter so as not to forget them. The stories we plan to share and others we choose not to. I look at those students and I gauge the distance that separates their journey from mine. Two exiles that do not follow the same track. Not the same fears. Not the same flavour.

After your jump, silence. Your form, alone, in the

water. Far from people's eyes. A dot that floats, vanishes, then surfaces again. How long does that impression last, the sense that you don't exist, that you have never existed for the world around you? One, two, three minutes? How long does it take to be snuffed out like a mere reflection in the waters of an ancient city?

From the refugees' stories, we could create a sort of dictionary of our collective defeat. Each day, a face, a name or an image would add to it. For now, I return to my notebook to add the name of your compatriot, Fatim the woman footballer. She dreamed of a professional career in Italy. She played for a club in Serrekunda, fourteen kilometres from Banjul. She was also the goalkeeper for the Gambian national under-seventeens team. In February 2016, she set out for Libya. Eight months later, she tried to make the crossing. A storm wiped out her dream. All the Italian football grounds have ended up at the bottom of the Mediterranean. An inaccessible marine paradise. The sea stole Fatim's gloves. All that remains is her frozen smile on a large-format photo carried by her brother Momodou. Sitting on a threadbare carpet, her mother prays in silent grief.

My nose pressed to the window of the airport bus, I brood over the sadness of the Parisian streets. I know this journey by heart, having made it many times, but right now, everything seems different. The Parc Montsouris looks like a vast walled cemetery. The Charléty stadium is a sort of ugly, shapeless saucer. People are ambling along the tram lines. A couple at a bus stop are showing signs of impatience. When it starts to rain, I realise that something alienates me from this city. The stirrings of a definitive rupture. This trip to Venice feels like an unjustified escape. I try to stifle the question that keeps coming back. What am I going to Venice to seek?

It is from the Bridge of the Barefoot Monks that people would first have spotted you. Unless it was the passengers on the packed vaporetto that passed within a few metres of you. Or perhaps those curious onlookers waiting at the Ferrovia stop. Or again, the tourists sitting on the terrace of the Carlton Hotel. Little does it matter. Why insist on solving the mystery of the first person to see your foreigner's body? All those eyes were certainly not expecting to see your head and arms in the water. All those baffled, embarrassed, and at first maybe even amused looks, prompted by your intrusive presence.

What does a person do when it's time to leave, when the journey of exile ceases to be an obsessive dream and becomes a reality of fire and fear? What do they choose to take with them when they travel with fear in their belly? I come across the story of the young Malian who had sewn his school report inside his jacket. We know what happens next. The sinking of the trawler in the Mediterranean. A forensic pathologist finds the report when trying to identify the body. A report for a deferred admission. Grades for a new school year that will not happen. The sunken boat is an empty classroom. With no furniture. No students. No curriculum. Only the silence of the depths and, by way of a legacy, a list of good grades in a fourteen-year-old boy's school report.

The big blue signs indicate that we are almost at Orly airport. My gaze hovers over the aisle of the bus as I continue to wonder what I hope to find in Venice, almost four years after your death. I end up convincing myself that writing is a mere pretext, a way of filling the vacuum, breaking the silence and fleshing out a disjointed story that refuses closure. A story essentially of borders. Where does your tragedy end and the shame of the world begin? I can no longer bear my compulsion to add questions on top of questions. I always return to the same point. As if your death defies reason, resists the act of reconstruction. But actually, what is there to reconstruct?

After the stares come the shouts and screams. I read that cries broke out from all sides, resonating for a while across the Grand Canal as if in a vast echo chamber. Cries that were more or less spontaneous. Cries of panic or surprise, suspicion or alarm. Raucous or strident shouts, screams very quickly muffled by the façades or drowned out by the purring of engines. Cries to put an end to your disturbing presence, to drive away the prospect of a ruined holiday or an interrupted promenade.

Patch up the names. Sew up the holes in the stories.

I recall the interview with the forensic pathologist working to name the drowned and return their identity documents to them. Her name is Cristina and she works in a laboratory in Milan. I'm struck by the softness of her voice when she speaks of the young Malian boy. I wonder why she doesn't mention his first name or his surname. She says that in his jacket she found his blood-donor card and his library card. Two cards and a school report for an anonymous life.

On leaving the bus at Terminal 1, I feel as if I'm leaving Paris, as if I'm divesting myself of a burden that had become unbearable. I've always loved the atmosphere of airports. The chaotic, heady jumble of bodies, screens, adverts, shops, lights, escalators, cordons, entrance and exit control gates, vast stained-glass windows, suspended cables, CCTV cameras, announcements repeated time and time again, last calls before departure. The entire airport circus which you escaped.

In your field of vision is the forest of poles jutting out of the water like needles in your skin. Those *paline* as they are called in Venice are for mooring the boats. For you, they are simply wooden forms dancing on the edge of the precipice. Perhaps you notice that the ones in front of the Carlton are decorated. Pretty stripes that remind you of other poles that you had seen at the station exit. Then everything fades. The water rises and your body goes under again.

Apparently, diaries and drawings have been found in the clothing of other drowned migrants. Slices of life condensed into a line, a page, a notebook. I wonder whether you were in the habit of writing or drawing in Italy, whether you sometimes took notes, made sketches or diagrams. It is as if I have a visceral need to cling to something that had come from your fingers.

On the TV are endless reports of the regular floods in Venice. Procession of rubber boots. Installation of raised walkways. The persistence of the tourists who carry on taking selfies in the rain. Some are wearing brightly coloured plastic ponchos. A rainbow of faceless people impatient to tick off their list of must-visit places. I see them walking in single file. I switch channels. The rainbow vanishes, replaced by the row of body bags on a Greek beach. A brilliant blue sky and spring sunshine for another group of faceless people who travelled without any sort of list.

The first witnesses were confused. A few metres from you, a hand grips the rail of a vaporetto. Nearby, a finger points to the surface of the water. After the pointing and shouting, I wonder whether it occurred to anyone to take action.

At the departure gate, there's something disconcerting about the calm of the passengers. Visibly they've prepared for their trip. Compact bags. Sunglasses pushed back. Cameras slung over their shoulders. Some are holding guidebooks: *Three days in Venice*, *A Romantic Weekend in Venice*, *A Venice Holiday Guide*, *Venice for Families*. I wonder whether there's a guide to Venice for the solo visitor whose head is heavy, his mind haunted by a tragedy that refuses to go away.

I continue to think that there's something deceptive about Venice. As if each of the city's monuments were an image of itself, a dubious replica, an inexact copy. I wonder whether this absurd thought crossed your mind. Supposing Venice were a cardboard stage set.

The refugee's travel kit is like an extension of their body, a prolongation of their memory. I read an article about those fleeing Syria. A different geography, the same wounds. The same fragmented stories, filled with fear and uncertainty. The photos are arresting. Personal items can be seen among the nervous smiles. Spread out on crumpled towels. Mobile phones, chargers, tubes of toothpaste, creams, medicines, syringes, nappies, USB sticks, a change of clothes, pairs of shoes, cartons of milk, biscuits, SIM cards, banknotes, bracelets. Each object is a beam of light sweeping the refugee's path. I recall your backpack, the final spark before the lights went out.

The plane window offers a view of a world that you never saw. On the tarmac, baggage handlers are busy loading the last suitcases. As each one disappears, I feel as if I'm distancing myself a little further from the capital.

The captain's voice does not sound very reassuring. For the first time, I notice the clouds scudding faster across what looks like a vast blanket full of holes. It could begin to rain any moment now. I wonder what the weather will be like in Venice and whether it's wise to go there at this time of year. I immediately regret that thought, telling myself that there's something obscene about my anxiety.

The reports repeat that at first, "no one realised what was happening". As if you'd caught them all off guard. As if you'd shaken up their certainties, their points of reference, their fixed images of the famous city of the Doges. They may well have rubbed their eyes or scratched their heads; no one expected to see a young Gambian in the Grand Canal. Then, all of a sudden, it must have dawned on them.

In his little backpack, a Syrian kid had brought sweets with him. Marshmallows wrapped in a plastic bag. Childhood treats to sweeten the bitterness of the world.

As the plane took off, I glanced furtively at a group of tourists sitting at the back. They were talking in loud voices, trying to outdo one another with their plans for the trip, the palaces to visit, the restaurants to avoid, the must-sees. By the time they'd finished, I had the impression that they'd exhausted Venice before even setting foot there. After take-off, I reclined my seat and closed my eyes in an attempt to sleep.

Some people's imaginations made them think that you were joking, that you were playing a prank in the water, that you were an actor, a comedian, a player in search of inspiration, that you were seeking to attract attention through an improvised performance on Venice's watery stage.

In March 2020, the United Nations website announced that the migrant death toll in the Mediterranean had reached the milestone of 20,000. It took the umpteenth boat to capsize off the Libyan coast. I realised how cruel the word "milestone" is. The language of records and statistics that nothing seemed able to halt. The shocking numbers that haphazardly swallow up the individual faces, stories, journeys and fears, and the ordeal of those who leave and of those who stay behind. Abruptly, I realise that you are not one of the 20,000. Even in the infallible world of figures, you are reduced to the margins.

After reclining my seat, I scan the headlines of the newspaper I bought in Paris. The words dance before my eyes: "election night", "tax fraud", "voter turnout", "nuclear testing", "Tour de France"... On page ten, a sidebar mentions a dinghy capsizing off the coast of Libya. Five or six lines, then on to something else.

Among the first shouts that reach your ears from the Bridge of the Barefoot Monks, you can clearly hear the word "Africa". And there you are, carrying the continent or its image on your shoulders. Atlas in flesh and blood supporting that distant Africa, so little known that we continue to look at it through the lens of official reports, of leftovers from the colonial era, enduring fantasies fed by exotic photos and paternalistic attitudes. They shout "Africa" but they forget that you alone are a continent of emotions adrift.

How many Gambians before you had set foot on Italian soil? The question crushes the unbearable mass of articles that stream past, illustrated by those same photos showing men crammed together, arms dangling, eyes distraught, faces emaciated, waiting to be examined, checked, expelled, thrown out, sent back to those fringes where the cruellest hopes are born, where the yearning to leave is revived, those territories that exude discontent transmitted from one generation to the next, those familiar labyrinths, but whose escape route is always uncertain, where fantasies and monsters jostle. How many lives must be offered up to the lagoons to put an end to centuries of humiliation?

The flight attendant who stops beside me looks drawn. She tries to smile, but I very quickly see that she can't take any more of these back-to-back shuttle flights timed to the minute. Between flights, does she even have the time to visit Venice? During a stopover, might she have heard about you? I'm dying to ask her the question, but I soon realise that would be ridiculous. I put the glass of orange juice down on the tray table and let my gaze roam down the aisle. Everything is quiet. I try to go back to sleep, but the aircon is too noisy. I could start up a conversation with the woman on my right, but I notice the air pods in her ears and think better of it.

Then suddenly people are yelling to throw you a lifebelt or a life jacket. The difference matters little because eventually people see that you have no strength, that Venice is crushing you under the combined weight of its bridges, canals and palaces, and its myths negating your presence, reducing your breath to light convulsive tremors, drowned by the sound of the vaporetto passing a few metres from you in slow motion, as in a fading dream.

The stories of your fellow countrymen gather around your name forming a guard of honour around your wounded memory. On the Equal Times website, I read the story of Lamin, aged thirty-four, another Gambian refugee in Italy. Back home, he was the driver for an army officer implicated in the attempted coup of 30 December 2014. After the failure of the putsch, he describes how he had to drive the officer to the Senegalese border and abandon the idea of returning home for fear of his life. The rest is the story of yet another journey northwards: Senegal, Niger, Libya. In Italy, Lamin discovered a love of drawing. While waiting for the interview that might enable him to be granted asylum, he recounts his journey with coloured pencils. On a blank sheet of paper, he draws a boat crammed with terrified faces and closely surveilled by the shadow of a helicopter.

The captain announces that we're about to land, but the woman on my right has her eyes glued to her phone. The sun's rays through the window light up her doll's face. She scrolls through the photos with her thumbs at dizzying speed. Every so often, her thumb pauses then resumes its frantic scrolling. On that photo of you doing the rounds online, your gaze is contemplative, almost absent, dominating your discreet moustache and the pale blue of your shirt. Behind you, a slender tree against the gloomy sky.

After the shouts and cries for help, now comes the laughter, the jeering and the sniggering. People wonder what you're doing in the water. They call you an idiot because you don't know how to swim. That shameless way of finding the slightest pretext to brush you aside, point out your failings, nudge you that much closer to the void. You are mocked because your difference is a concentrate of all the things that they refuse to see.

Like Lamin, Omar doesn't show his face. In the photo alongside the article in *Le Monde*, he is gazing out of the bay window of a Parisian café. Before arriving in France, he lived in Brikama, thirty kilometres south of Banjul. A marriage refusal and threats when his sweetheart became pregnant drove him to leave the country. For a while, he lived in Casamance, then ended up in a port in

Mauritania. With other men disguised as construction workers, he travelled in the hold of a container ship. After a spell in Marseille, he managed to reach Paris. Like Lamin, Omar is waiting to be granted asylum. To kill time, he roams the streets of the capital and visits the sights. He says: "I would take RER A and go to the end of the line, Cergy, Torchy, and then I'd come back… It passed the time. I had nothing better to do". I know line A of the RER very well, having been a regular commuter between La Varenne-Chennevières and La Défense from 2008 and 2011. All of a sudden, I can picture the anonymous silhouettes of those wandering in the RER, dozing on the fold-up seats or against the windows, all those empty or evasive gazes caught in the wan light of the carriages. How many times did Omar make that journey back and forth? What did the RER mean to him other than the awful mirror of his journey, two fixed markers, two interchangeable points on the rails of a life on hold?

A few moments before landing, I stare out of the window. From the expanse of greenish water, branches appear, becoming part of the dry land. At the entrance to the lagoon are smoking chimneys, storage tanks, industrial buildings – some arranged in parallel rectangles, and others perpendicular. In the distance, is the brick-red of the Mestre and Marghera districts. Liberty Bridge snakes across the lagoon, dividing it in two. Venice is only visible from the opposite side of the plane. I am almost relieved.

Those few minutes that separate you from the other bank are an eternity. You have the sensation that the water is dragging at you a little harder and you wonder whether the nearby vaporetto will stop, or at least slow down. What thoughts are going round in your mind at that precise moment? Maybe you're not thinking about anything in particular. Simply that in-between state when you realise that it's too late to go back.

In 2016, after the election of the new Gambian president, some European politicians were quick to declare that Gambia was about to become "a safe country once more". Many Gambian refugees, especially in Germany, were afraid their asylum applications would be refused. Those men who had started new lives in the host countries did not want to return. To do so would be a step backwards, a leap into the unknown and precariousness.

When the plane lands on the tarmac of Marco Polo airport, I feel slightly tense. As if I were expecting to discover something that had been eluding me from the outset. As if I were finally going to go beyond the daunting mass of articles, reports and eyewitness accounts that I'd read so far. The group seated at the back has grown rowdy again. Their irritating laughter fills the plane. At one point, they even start singing. For the first time, the woman on my right speaks to me and asks if I've been to Venice before. I tell her I haven't and that is only my second time in Italy after a short trip to Florence in 2016. She smiles and says: "I love Florence. There's something captivating about that city, something…" She pauses, then adds, almost in a whisper: "…poetic." I ask her if she's travelling alone and she says she's visiting friends, a French couple who have been living in Venice for more than five years. She adds: "What about you? What brings you here?" I reply at once: "I'm trying to write a book about a man that Venice may have already forgotten."

How many lifebelts were thrown to you? Two, three or four? Apparently, they all fell within a few centimetres of you. You could simply have reached out and grabbed the nearest one. But how could you reach out when your entire body was numb, the freezing water penetrating your every pore? Then the abuse grew even harsher: "Let him die!" For others, you'd do better to "go back home". The brutal cynicism that persisted in denying your presence.

You had no choice. Those who leave do not always have the choice. I recall the incredible story in April 2019 of the stowaway who hid in the undercarriage of a plane flying from Pointe-à-Pitre to Cayenne, with a refuelling stop in Fort-de-France, Martinique. When the man emerged, dressed in rags, he was dazed, stupefied by the 1600 kilometres he'd just travelled. In an online video, he can be seen stumbling towards an airport employee, removing what look like earplugs and trying to exchange a few words with her. Another member of staff shouts:

"Who are you? Where have you come from?" Then he asks his colleague to call the police. The man stands there, covered in soot, his gaze vacant. What exactly is he thinking? Will he manage to find words to explain his extreme journey?

In the arrivals hall I look for exit 2 to catch the blue ATVO express bus to Piazzale Roma. It's a twenty-minute or so ride. I'm in no hurry, but I don't want to waste time. Once there, I planned to drop off my backpack at the hotel and then carry out an initial recce of the scene of the tragedy. I say "recce" but I don't know whether, four years after the event, there'll be any trace. The airport is surprisingly quiet. Nothing to report other than large posters of Venice landmarks along the travelators and two giant lingerie ads framing the departures and arrivals boards. In the ads, two women are arching their backs in a sexy, provocative pose. I wonder whether Venice tourism really needs this kind of showcase.

According to some eyewitnesses, a lifeguard was about to dive in to try and rescue you but was dissuaded. After all, he wasn't equipped. He didn't have the protective black rubber wetsuit or the certainty that he could or should help you. Apparently, one or two tourists were also prepared to jump off the vaporetto to help. Others felt it would be too risky since the water temperature was five degrees. Insults started flying again. The nauseating words drummed out. People would rather see you die here, now, as fast as possible, so they can quickly turn the page of this unforeseen interruption and put an end to this misadventure. Let them fish your lifeless body out so that peace and tranquillity can be restored. As if nothing had happened.

Writing is an echoing of stubborn questions. Each one opens a floodgate of images that flow from your story, widens the circle of indignation and disgust. As I read, this question keeps coming back to me: how does a person survive a journey in the undercarriage of a plane? One article informs me that in July 2019, a man "fell from the sky" into a south London garden. He was a Nairobi airport employee who had just travelled from Nairobi to London huddled in the undercarriage of a Kenya Airways plane, where food, water and a bag were found. The man would have died well before the landing gear was lowered. He had frozen to death at 10,000 metres altitude. He hadn't had the chance to set foot in Heathrow Airport. He plummeted like a stone in front of the homeowner who was sunbathing in his garden.

When the paunchy driver started up the bus with a weary sigh, for the first time I felt pleased at the idea of being in Venice. I think of you again. If you'd had the choice, you might not have opted for Italy. You would have preferred England, Germany or a Scandinavian country. Head north, where the bureaucracy is reputed to be more lenient. But you had to follow the path of others. There was no room for originality. The other day, before booking my ticket, I checked the flights between Banjul and Venice. As if I wanted to invent a different journey for you, the one you weren't able to make, that you would never have been able to make. One journey to obliterate the other. A journey as it ought to be, with a valid passport, a stamped visa, labelled luggage and stars in your eyes.

I end up watching the video. On the deck of the vaporetto, the passengers clustered together are hazy, insubstantial shapes. Who are they? Where do they come from? Are there as many tourists as locals among them? Are they the captive witnesses of an umpteenth tragedy or the designated culprits of a fresh crime? And the coincidence of their presence at that exact moment, in front of you, faced with the evidence of your death, the proof of your last movements, the final gasps of your body overpowered by the water. A dozen men and women confronted with the face of death prowling, ready to strike.

At another time, your country was a refuge for others, come mainly from Sierra Leone, Liberia and Senegal. Follow the movement of those seeking refuge from political strife or civil wars. Reverse the possibilities. Learn to see your country in both directions. Departures and arrivals.

Through the window of the bus as it picks up speed on the Via Orlanda, I grow used to the utter dreariness of the scenery. Car parks and petrol stations. Occasionally, by the roadside, a two- or three-storey house, a church or a restaurant. A little further, fenced off or gated residential neighbourhoods. Then, regularly, as far as the eye can see, vast abandoned fields overgrown with brambles or scrub. The Venice sky is low and grey. The postcard is a mental image.

For the first time, I realise that you had in front of you the three flags of the Hotel Carlton: those of the Veneto, Italy and the EU. During all that time, the three flags were fluttering a few metres from you. Three geographies to pinpoint your last journey. Three bands, twelve stars and a winged lion to illuminate the long tunnel taking you to the other shore.

Relieve the searing pain of your death in the smile of Ibrahim in Cyprus. In front of the louvred green shutters, like Lamin and Omar, he's waiting for the result of his asylum application. On the InfoMigrants website, the story of his journey is just like the others: Gambia, Senegal, Mali, Niger, Libya. Having set sail for Italy, he and some sixty other men end up in Cyprus. He knows nothing about the island. He manages to build a new life there. He works in a carob factory, studies information technology and plays the djembe. There's something infectious about his radiant smile in the photos. In the midst of the graffiti adorning the Cypriot streets, his drum beats out your release.

On Liberty Bridge, I manage to make out the island of San Secondo through the haze. Apparently, from the eleventh century, it was home to a Benedictine convent which was succeeded by the Dominicans. It was later converted to a powder-keg store. Nowadays, the ruined buildings are surrounded by dense, bushy vegetation. There is something disturbing about this deserted island at the gates of Venice. I've always been strangely fascinated by ruined landscapes where concern for preserving a trace vies with the erasure of the site.

I count eleven balconies on the main façade of the Hotel Carlton. Is there someone watching you from a distance as your arms continue to vanish and reappear on the surface of the water? Do the cries for help reach the ears of the guests eating at the outdoor tables? Is the vendor from the kiosk opposite the hotel aware of what's happening behind him? So many questions that close over you, slowly, like one more trap with no way out.

From one smile to the next, reconstitute the face of the country in exile. Piece together scraps of journeys torn from resignation. Continue the patient gathering of names and stories. My research takes me to Bologna, 150 kilometres south of Venice where a young Gambian plays for the city's football team. His name is Musa and like so many others, he left Libya on an inflatable dinghy. Like you, he couldn't swim, but a humanitarian ship rescued him. An Italian couple then helped him obtain a professional footballer licence. He started out with

Chievo Verona before joining Bologna FC. On 5 July 2020, he scored his first goal against Inter Milan at San Siro. I replay his goal but I have the feeling that his long victory slide is also a way of warding off ill luck once and for all.

In the distance, the red roofs of Venice. The bus driver gives another sigh. The fog has dispersed a little and at last I can see the surface of the water, almost clearly, like a vast, endless mirror where the five letters of your name are reflected. The passengers are starting to get excited. Some are already on their feet, their noses pressed to the windows. With their blissful smiles and their affected postures, they look ridiculous. I prefer to look away towards the lagoon.

What if this entire tragedy were down to the fatal time lag between your actions and people's reactions? I can imagine the hesitation of some, the incomprehension of others, the awkwardness that descends like a lead weight paralysing any kind of response. And meanwhile, your body is still trapped in the Grand Canal. A confrontation that is necessarily unequal.

It was in the streets of Bakoteh, a district in Serrekunda, that Ebrima first kicked a football. Like Fatim and Musa, he dreamed of matches under the floodlights. InfoMigrants reports that he was barely fourteen when he joined the procession of those heading northwards. In Libya, when evening fell over the camp, at the hour when insults fly thick and fast and the horror erupts, he thinks of his mother, his two sisters and his brother back home. Like you, he lands in Sicily, weak but relieved. The promise of a new life to be built. Later, he's taken in by a family in Rieti, close to Rome. At the foot of the mountain, he heals from his Libyan wound and waits for his chance. He plays for the local club, where he's soon scouted and transferred to AS Roma. In 2019, he signs his first contract as a professional footballer. Nearly two years later, Ebima plays his first official match for the Rome team. After that, it's the hymn of the Champions League, the emotion of a footballer playing for a top European club and the pride of his mother who receives a share of his salary.

When I alight at Piazzale Roma, I have the impression that my bag is almost empty. It's late afternoon and a light wind is blowing over Venice. I take a few photos of the square. From that moment on, I know that I will have to document everything. Most importantly, steer clear of the stream of tourists pouring into the city. Stay aloof. Avoid intrusive or curious gazes. As I wander through the streets around the square, I pass the People Mover shuttle stop where you can get the monorail to Tronchetto for the ferry to the Lido. A man in his sixties, no doubt intrigued by my comings and goings and perhaps also by my unusual appearance, comes over to me. He says a few words in Italian, which I don't understand. Thinking that I'm lost, he points to Constitution Bridge, which leads to the railway station.

As if he were reminding me of the reason for my trip and putting me back on the trail of your journey.

According to a few eyewitnesses, you made what looked like a final gesture in trying to grab one of the lifebelts. Your left or right arm outstretched to seize the last object that could have kept you alive or at least offered you a little respite. Some wondered why your attempt was so feeble and half-hearted. They even saw it as a form of indecisiveness. They're forgetting that your body is now frozen stiff, that the first shivers have given way to slow, halting, breathing, that your fingers have turned blue, your ribcage has suddenly contracted, your pulse is more irregular than ever and you are perhaps beginning to feel drowsy, a sort of general wooziness that's spreading like an unstoppable tumour, hampering your final reflexes.

Not far from the Italian border, Musa, second row Gambian player for Briançon rugby club, is threatened with expulsion. A temporary player's permit guaranteed him nothing. He needed to work. The club made every effort to help him. Since his arrival in France from Italy, he's had one job after another, in construction, cleaning or security. Each day, Musa and his wife wake up to a horrendous memory. The body of their one-year-old daughter who had drowned when they crossed the Mediterranean. That budding life wrenched from them, stolen, carried off in a flood of tears and screams. On 22 December 2020, almost three years after your death, Musa's smile is on the front page of *Le Dauphiné*. He's holding the oval ball as if he'll never let go. The snow falling over Briançon tastes of resilience and the refusal to give up.

As I climb the first steps of Constitution Bridge, I know that I'm nearing the scene of the tragedy. I feel a pang at the thought of discovering Venice as you saw it one afternoon in January 2017. On the bridge, I fight my way through the people climbing up and down the steps. Apparently, this iron-and-glass bridge has been the subject of controversy since it was built in 2008. The Venetians considered it too modern, and some compared it to a hideous lobster spoiling the "authentic" beauty of their city. Lost in my thoughts, I realise at the last minute that I must make way for a porter pushing his luggage cart past. A little farther on, I move out of the way again to avoid an Alsatian on a lead being walked by its owner. I decide to stop. From the bridge, the leafy trees of the Papadopoli Gardens exude a vague sense of calm. As if your memory were there, gracious, intact, preserved at the tip of a crackling branch or a trembling leaf.

At what point, numbed to the core, do you lose consciousness? That moment when no more shivers run through your body. Just tiny, imperceptible tremors, at intervals, moving inevitably towards silence. In the calm bed of the Grand Canal, a door might open at any moment to welcome your solitary traveller's soul.

All those men betrayed by false promises, swindled

down to the depths of their pockets and their hearts, scapegoats left to the gratuitous violence of the times. On 22 July 2005, you were ten years old and childhood was a rocky experience. That night, in Mbour, Senegal, some fifty Ghanaians set sail in a pirogue. They would never reach the smugglers' boat awaiting them off the Gambian coast. A night battling against the wild sea, trying to defeat the contrary winds of fate. Early next morning, their pirogue washed ashore off the coast of Banjul. The men were arrested, beaten up, imprisoned, accused of every wrong, suspected of plotting against the president of Gambia. Later, in a dense forest, their bodies were riddled with cowardly, murderous bullets. Three survivors would testify to the atrocity. One of them was called Martin. At the cemetery, he stood behind a commemorative plaque engraved with the following words: "In loving memory of the forty four Ghanaians who lost their lives under tragic circumstances in the Gambia in July 2005. May God Almighty grant them eternal rest."

I decide to carry on to the station. I'll drop my bag off at the hotel later. On the façade of the Palazzo Grandi Stazioni, the former Italian railway company headquarters acquired by the Veneto general council, the three flags are part of that network of symbols now permanently associated with your name. Veneto, Italy, Europe. Three spaces to drown bitterness and sing your requiem. The only way to give this journey a meaning is to write between the island, the lagoon and the continent.

Apparently a motoscafo passed within a few metres of you and could easily have stopped to rescue you. But it didn't. Some articles mention that the nearby boats did turn their engines off so as not to injure you with their blades. You see, Pateh, they were thinking of you. Your presence in the waters of the Grand Canal did not go unnoticed. As if you should be grateful and not expect anything more.

Since 2017 and the departure of President Jammeh, some of your fellow countrymen have returned home. The following year, the numbers returning voluntarily greatly increased. Like a fresh wind blowing over the lands of exile. I wonder what you would have done in 2018. Would the change of president have been enough to convince you? Was this a temporary respite or a lasting new dawn?

My research reveals that the first floor of the Palazzo Grandi Stazioni close to Santa Lucia station is home to the migration regulation offices. Part of the social services department, this body is in charge of "promoting and implementing initiatives to help overcome the specific difficulties associated with being an immigrant, to encourage the process of integration into the regional community and to work for the social, linguistic and professional inclusion of immigrant citizens from third countries and residing legally in Veneto." The words "integration", "community" and "inclusion" continue to resonate in my head. All of a sudden, this disturbing paradox strikes me: a stone's throw from the spot where you drowned, Italian officials were seeking to avoid this kind of tragedy.

Eventually, someone called 115. Eyewitnesses were already describing what had happened, sharing their versions with newcomers on the scene. While waiting for the emergency services, you are a topic of conversation, something to talk about by the water's edge.

On the other side, there are the bonds of solidarity, the daily lesson in fraternity, the hands outstretched across borders. The other day, I came across the Gambia-Helfernetz website, an online network bringing together voluntary and full-time supporters of Gambian refugees, mainly from Baden-Württemburg in Germany. The network is made up of aid and friendship groups, private initiatives and support from the towns and municipal councils. According to the website, there are some 20,000 Gambians in Germany, more than half of them in Baden-Württemburg. The network maintains confidentiality. A fraternal web woven in respect and kindness.

Slowly Venice opens up to my senses. Every sign, every symbol, every tremor of the lagoon is important. How many of St Mark's lions look at me in the four corners of the city? Whether it's holding a book or a sword, the lion is always in profile, its wings spread. Venetian tradition has it that when Mark was travelling through Europe, he arrived at a lagoon in Venice, whereupon an angel appeared to him and said, "Here, thy body will rest". As if, centuries in advance, that promise heralded fragments of your story. As if I needed to invent wings for you and offer you the flash of a sword or the substance of a book to live up to the legend.

And now a distant siren is wailing, muffled at first then becoming louder and louder, reaching the ears of the passengers on the vaporetto, which has been stationary for a while. Soon, the curtain will fall on this macabre scene and they will all be able to resume their chatter.

On the InfoMigrants website, I heal your wound in the smile of Yahya, a young Gambian who lives in Germany. A photo shows him standing in front of the coffin of a fellow Gambian about to be repatriated. From a village outside Stuttgart, Yahya runs a radio station in Banyul as well as WhatsApp groups to help Gambians in Germany with administrative formalities and social service applications. So, here are your brothers in exile organising the distribution of aid, fundraising, and running a programme of meetings and talks. Yahya would like to become a teacher. A music lover like Ibrahim, he sometimes plays in the village brass bands. Every so often, he recalls crossing the Mediterranean, the months of wandering around Milan, his fortuitous arrival in Germany. He makes video calls to his mother and is looking forward to the day when he'll be able to hug her again.

The map of verbal violence is constantly expanding, defiling what is left of your image, of your presence. On the deck of the vaporetto, passengers criticise one another for the way they recount your death over and over again, for the disgrace of having watched or allowed you to die, for the abuse hurled at you for no reason, for the need to put an end to the commotion so that traffic on the Grand Canal can resume and allow everyone to wriggle out of this situation as if extricating themselves from a tight garment that clings to the skin.

At the far end of the Palazzo Grandi Stazioni, I stop in front of a statue commemorating the railway workers of the Veneto region who fell during World War I. The inscription *Vobis Gloria Nobis Exemplum* (Glory to you, an example to us) stands out above the two bronze figures on a granite base. The soldier, naked, his head flung back, is supported by a woman draped in a garment and holding a shield in her left hand, as if to protect him. The sculpture has something of the tragic sacrifice about it. I question myself about the level of sacrifice in your story, about the meaning of that abandonment as much voluntary as forced, born as much from the accumulation of disappointments as from events running away with you. In front of the statue, I realise that everything I've written so far has been an attempt to flesh out the meandering, erratic substance of the story. The hard gravestone of this memorial in contrast to the fleeting reflections of your story.

All the journeys that would stay in the shadows if there weren't those pathfinders, those carriers of words and stories between the two shores. One of them is Ismail, an Anglo-Somali journalist. In June 2016, on the streets of Palermo, he met Babucarr, known as Taka. Another of your fellow countrymen who dreamed of a new life under the Italian sky. In a BBC report, Ismail tells how he had decided to visit Taka's family in Tujereng, western Gambia. He took with him photographs and recordings of Taka as if taking evidence to the family of a kidnap victim that they are still alive. In the meantime, Taka left Italy for Malta, where he was now working in a restaurant. When they were back in touch, Ismail gave Taka news of his family and stories he'd brought back from his trip to the Gambia. That way snippets of life circulate, easing both the sting of interrogations and the pain of separation.

For the first time, a sovereign silence seemed to reign over the Grand Canal, giving the impression that the city was frozen in mourning, that your body was now the new focal point. The only sounds were those of the vaporetto revving up its engine again or the plashing of a gondola moving off. Then everything seemed to stop when the boats of the *vigili del fuoco* arrived on the scene.

Here I am, almost four years after your death, outside Santa Lucia station. Porters are relaxing in the shade of the shrubs during the late-afternoon lull. In the little square to the right of the main entrance, a couple stand transfixed by the statue of the Immaculate Virgin. At the Ferrovia stop opposite, tourists queue to buy their tickets. The station building is like a concrete ocean liner docked in the Grand Canal. I remember reading that the station was built on the site of a church that was destroyed in 1861. It used to house the relics of Saint Lucia of Syracuse, which have since been transferred to the church of San Geremia. So it is with writing in the aftermath of your death. A transfer of relics that is reconstructed around your memory.

Between the gaps in the story is the image of that crowded ferry crossing River Gambia at the end of January 2017. After the autocrat had fled, it was bringing home the refugees who'd settled in Senegal. Those men and women running in the half-darkness so as not to miss the last departure for Banjul. Those children, pulling along their brightly coloured little suitcases, repatriating their dreams in small pieces. Those faces suddenly lit up at the long-awaited prospect of being reunited with their loved ones. Here and there, T-shirts appropriately bearing the slogan: "Gambia has decided".

The firefighters cordoned off the site of the tragedy. Change of scene. Reconfiguration of the space. Keeping the onlookers away. The red bands completed the process of isolating your body. Then, slowly, conversations started up again, first in whispers among the crowd, then voices that were increasingly strident. People answered the firefighters' questions as they gathered information and recovered your body. A pall descended over the

Grand Canal. A man had drowned in the waters of a city nearly 6,000 kilometres from his homeland.

On the station esplanade, in front of the row of lampposts, I thought about that Venice of long ago, the one you perhaps glimpsed on an advert or a tourist office poster. The Venice that no longer exists, that of Canaletto and Guardi, topographic views and geometric details, festivities and commemorations resuscitated on the banks of the Grand Canal. I decide to sit on the station steps for a few minutes. I open my backpack and without thinking, I take out my wallet. My plane ticket is there, with my passport and residence permit. For no reason, I re-read my name, my date of birth and the expiry date. I close my eyes and images flood my mind. The endless steps at Cité metro station in Paris. The Police Prefecture with its great gates, which opens at 8.35. The crowd of anxious, watchful foreigners waiting under the sloping roof. My folder with the certified copies of all my documents. The vague recollections of a novel I was reading while waiting for the gates to open and another that I was writing in the evenings, inspired by the oppressive, unbearable material of my day.

A ring of plastic bottles for a lifebelt and your memory that floats back up to the surface. Achraf is a sixteen-year-old Moroccan boy who along with thousands of others tries to cross the border with Spain at Sebta, in the north of Morocco. In May 2021, seeing that child crying in the water left me with a feeling of bitterness and shame. There is this video that I keep playing. Achraf's tears are needles piercing my heart. In front of him, the Spanish soldier who speaks to him in Arabic, tries to reassure him: "We're not going to hurt you". Relieved of his bottles, Achraf runs out of the water and desperately tries to clamber over a wall. Caught by the soldier, he continues to cry and repeats: "Please try to understand us. I don't want to go back." That is his third failed attempt to cross the border. Sent back to Morocco, eventually he is taken into the care of a charity that offers him job training. "Please try to understand us," said Achraf. That "us" that reverberates from Fnideq to Banjul, from Sebta to Venice. The "us" of that shared experience whose suffering knows neither bounds nor borders.

Around the Grand Canal, the only thing that shines are the fluorescent strips on the Venetian firefighters' jackets. The professional divers are now kitted out and ready to start the search for your body. You're somewhere on the bottom, inert, not breathing, your spirit flown to other lands. It will become known later that you have on your person the plastic wallet containing your train ticket and your residence permit.

Turning my back on the station, I head towards the Grand Canal. My backpack is surprisingly light. Reaching the water's edge, I sit down again and place my foot on a step. In front of me are the buildings I'd seen on the map. San Simeone Piccolo with its green bronze dome, the Antiche Figure hotel with its red banner and two balconies, the Hotel Carlton on the Grand Canal with its three flags and its panoramic terrace, and a little further along, the building of the Sisters of Mary Child with its flower-covered frontage, prefiguring the treetops of the Papadopoli Gardens at the end of the canal path. My gaze roves over the façades. I am reminded of the disturbing image of Lucia of Syracuse bearing a dish containing her eyes. I wonder to what extent writing can bear your gaze, advance like a torch through the dark tangle of your tragedy. I have never felt so keenly the anguish of the labyrinth and the weight of your presence.

From one gaze to the next, when words and speeches fall silent, rises the supreme power of the image. In the multimedia library of Uzès, in the south of France, the journalist and war photographer Édouard exhibits photos that he took in 2016 on board the *Aquarius*, the SOS Méditerranée boat that saves lives off the coast of Libya. His photos speak of the growing dread, the silence that kills and the screams that burst out in the dawn light. He had been kidnapped in Syria and experienced the refugee camps in Türkiye and Myanmar. He had chosen the chaos of conflict over the calm of his native village, Saint-Quentin-la-Poterie, six kilometres from Uzès. I know the area from having lived and studied there from 2004 to 2008. I remember the poetic names of the villages around Alès which I used to cycle through: Saint-Hilaire-de-Brethmas, Saint-Privat-des-Vieux, Saint-Martin-de-Valgalgues. My early years in France had the flavour of the fields and the disused coal mines.

I realise that Édouard's photos are in black and white. In one of them, a man photographed from behind and wearing a Puma T-shirt has his palms raised in a gesture that could equally be one of prayer or of disappointment. His gaze is fixed on an inflatable dinghy during a rescue operation. In another photo, men sitting or lying down, are wrapped in blankets. One is hiding his face in his hands. I wish I could have been a photographer – pictures are so much more eloquent than words.

The divers did the job. Between the firefighters' red boats, behind the line of gondolas, can be seen the little ladder that will be used to bring up your body, already sealed in a blue bag. The operation continues. Four firefighters hoist it up. Two others watch the scene. Now, they are pushing the body bag under the gaze of the onlookers herded behind the red cordon. Later, the dispersed crowd will rewrite your story on the restaurant terraces, in the narrow winding streets or under the bridges. The Grand Canal will once more be teeming with boats and people.

All of a sudden, beside the water, I experience a bout of giddiness. A cacophony of images, names, places and descriptions creates a sort of invisible noose that tightens around my throat. Only your face is there, clear and luminous, like an apparition repeated endlessly. I can no longer hear anything except the twitching of a human body plunging into the darkness. Venice is a vast planet that explodes into a thousand pieces. Around me, the world dissolves and again I have that impulsive urge to shout until the sky splits open. I open my mouth, but no sound comes out. Gradually, the earth gives way beneath me and I feel as if I'm toppling into the water.

PART THREE

THE WORDS

A morning like any other. Hurried footsteps in the corridor. Someone clearing their throat. Snatches of conversation in Italian or English. Every so often, a door bangs or a window squeaks. Nothing has changed since yesterday. Rays of light filter through the louvred shutters. The day is dawning in this hotel room where I've broken off from months of investigation. Now, I can write it all down. I've lost track of time. I no longer know how many days it is since the accident. All I know is that on the day I arrived in Venice, I experienced a giddy spell beside the water, close to the station. Lack of sleep, tiredness from the journey, the huge amount of reading and the abundance of material I've amassed on the subject of your drowning and the anguish it created had overwhelmed me. I ended up thinking that the Grand Canal wanted to punish me for my excessive, misplaced curiosity. I should not have delved into your story. It's never good to poke around in ashes.

Everyone talks about the tragedy. The Venice public prosecutor opened an investigation to determine whether there had been any "negligence". Later, people might say that "the investigation revealed new elements" or that "it is following its course". From now on, you are entirely at the mercy of language.

Did the world see you as the refugee, the Gambian, the African or the Black man? All four at once, perhaps? Your drowning had become the meeting point of all those identities that people were eager to brandish one by one and, depending on the circumstances, all those labels people stuck on you and unstuck at will, each with its repeated clichés and shorthand. They found it hard to admit that they were seeking, perhaps unconsciously, a way of containing the waves created by your tragedy.

I don't know how I ended up at the hotel opposite the station, on the other bank of the Grand Canal. Perhaps that's where I'd booked a room. As I did every morning, I lay on my bed and stared at the wallpaper. I felt as if I was locked in a cage and had lost the key.

I imagine the disjointed statements of the eyewitnesses being given at one of the city's police stations, maybe the one at Piazzale Roma. Your story is a heavy burden which the whole of Venice is keen to shrug off. The circumstances of your arrival, the significance of your last actions, the nature of the screams, the truth of the insults, the description of that final scene, recounted, questioned, analysed, reinterpreted a hundred times. Everything has to be written down in halting half-sentences that will end up in a file on a carabiniere's computer, read later by a senior officer, forwarded to other departments for rubber-stamping, included in official reports and distributed to whomsoever it may concern.

How many writers have lost their memories on the terraces of this city? How many Venice lovers, dreamers, celebrities, nonentities have drowned their sorrows in the waters of the Grand Canal? How is it possible to write about Venice after Alfred de Musset and Madame de Staël, Balzac and Proust, Ruskin and Hemingway? How can I compete with this Venice literature of myth and intrigue?

From my hotel room window, my eyes seek out the exact spot where you drowned. Your memory is an easy prey and the Grand Canal looks like a long, scaly, green reptile about to devour it.

After your body was fished out, the story did the rounds of the press, social media and news websites. Almost everywhere, you were the "migrant" who had survived the arduous journey across the desert and the Mediterranean to die in the calm waters of the Grand Canal. This inclination to dwell on the absurd, paradoxical, almost fatal nature of your story. After all, paradox is easier to stomach than the brutal, naked truth of violence.

When I have no more energy to write, I rip out blank pages from my notebook and draw boats of all shapes and sizes. I give each one the name of one of the women or men I've encountered in my research. Then I read their names out loud, one after the other, like passwords to help me cross borders and knock down walls, like rallying cries that I shout to a crowd of invisible readers.

Standing at the window, I think I recognise a shadow between the striped poles jutting out of the water. I follow the movement of a form that's pacing up and down in front of the station. My gaze returns to the flower pots hanging from the balcony to the right of my room, then to the three flags on the left fluttering on the hotel façade. As I do every morning, I spend a while doing nothing, with no other aim but to watch the place where you took your bow. Each morning, I feel the need to cling to a view, an image, a sign that evokes your presence.

There is talk of "failure to assist a person in danger". Seen in that light, everything seems disconcertingly simple. You were in danger of your life. People should have done everything possible to come to your aid. The rest is just idle talk

One of the most frequent sources of information is the *Corriere del Veneto*. I come across an online article about you and I'm intrigued by the readers' comments. Often one can learn a great deal from reading these. I translate and copy some of them into my notebook:

"Rescuing a drowning man is an obligation according to maritime law."

"A lot of fuss about nothing."

"Human life is too precious to endanger it, even for a noble cause."

"Apart from children and the elderly, all those who were present are to blame."

"It's one thing to throw oneself into the freezing waters of the Grand Canal in January, and it's another to write articles from the warmth of one's sitting room."

"I wouldn't jump into the Grand Canal in January, not even to save my wife, as we'd probably both die and our children would be orphans. He wanted to die, let's not blame others!"

"I am profoundly convinced that if a dog had fallen into the canal, more than one person would have dived in… and now they'd be guests on all the daytime TV shows."

"We couldn't do more to help the invaders if we tried."

On a side wall in the hotel's breakfast room, there's a Venetian mask that stares at me with its two disturbing black holes. In the morning, I drink my coffee in one go. Guests queue at the buffet. They are calm and orderly. They hold their white plates, ready to serve themselves from the spread on the long table covered in a white cloth. Here, everything is a pristine, dazzling white, almost offensive.

I go back to this basic fact: the investigation will reveal nothing, or little of your past life. It will not be able either to establish the private reasons for your action or the unspoken pain of your death. In the investigators' final report, there will be neither your last thoughts in front of the crowd, nor the jumbled images in the heads of the witnesses and the spectators.

No matter how hard I try to avoid books written by others, I always end up seeking refuge in their words as I try to grasp this Venice that eludes me. Hemingway wrote that Venice "is a good town to walk in […] It's a strange, tricky town and to walk from any part to any other given part of it is better than working crossword puzzles." I don't like crossword puzzles, but I ought perhaps to get out of the hotel and learn to wander around the city. Hemingway stayed at the Gritti Palace, ate fish bought at the Rialto market and had an affair with a young Venetian woman. I ask myself what we have in common.

In the hotel lobby, there are wide armchairs upholstered in padded velvet, gilded coffee tables, vases with yellow flowers on long, slender stalks. On the floor, the white-and-gold checkered tiling makes me feel as if all this is a game. As if I'm playing at trying to piece together your story. Playing at stringing words together to put out the fire of the collective culpability. Playing shamelessly at the roulette of belated and fundamentally useless homage.

Another Venetian newspaper, *La Nuova di Venezia e Mestre*, reports that apparently the authorities pressed charges against the young driver of the motoscafo that passed close to you without offering help. He should at least have slowed down. His attitude contravened maritime law. I wonder what went through the head of that young man, whether his gaze met yours, whether a thought crossed his mind, whether his hand trembled, whether the sight of your body disappearing and reappearing had any effect on him. I think of that unexpected encounter between two young men in the waters. Him heading for Venice casino and you quitting life through the gate of the Grand Canal.

It struck me that after that 22 January 2017, the famous saying "See Venice and die" would never mean the same again.

I saw her one evening on the hotel terrace. She was reading a book and every so often she'd pause and look up to admire the dome of San Simeone Piccolo. It was the first time that I'd gone up to the terrace. The tables were laid for dinner. There was a young couple on the far side and an elderly man who was staring in the direction of Constitution Bridge. I had my notebook with me so I sat down at a table not far from her and began to make notes. It was she who spoke to me first. She asked me if I was a writer. I said no, but she appeared not to believe me. I realised that she was keen to start up a conversation. Her name was Alma and she was waiting for a male friend who was supposed to be meeting her in Venice in a few days' time. She had a strange gaze, a mixture of sadness and gentleness. The book she was reading was *Le Roman de Venise*. She whispered that it was the correspondence between George Sand and Alfred de Musset, and that it also included notes, poems and documents relating to their stay in Venice in 1834. She added: "I like love stories that end with a break-up." Then she resumed her reading.

According to online sources, the investigators have access to five videos shot on the day you drowned. Four of them are by amateurs and the fifth is footage from the municipal CCTV camera. Five angles to give a semblance of coherence to your tragedy, to fill in some gaps and possibly offer some tentative answers.

In the immense library of writings about Venice, there are characters beguiled by dreams and others by illusion, boats steered by skilful drivers, windows open onto short-lived love affairs and unsolved crimes, tilted hats and others held out to passers-by, masks worn on nights of the full moon, songs strummed beneath the bridges, servants forgotten between the pages of novels, porters with slightly bowed shoulders, guards disguised at the gates of palaces, snooty maître d's and heavily made-up courtesans, epochs and stories bound by the malleable stuff of myth. A vast field of ruins in which destiny has planted your name.

Alma and I had got into the habit of meeting on the hotel terrace every evening before sunset. Delighted to keep each other company but both deeply absorbed. She in the steamy letters of George Sand and Alfred de Musset, and I in my notes scattered into a thousand fragments. Between us, the soothing silence, and above our heads, the spellbinding green of the dome. Every so often, I get up to watch the station esplanade. I sometimes glimpse a silhouette walking hesitantly in the direction of the Bridge of the Barefoot Monks. I don't know whether it's a hallucination or whether I keep reliving your arrival in Venice.

A comment on the website of *Le Parisien* says that you would have been "much better off" in your village, surrounded by the "strong support" of your family, rather than "isolated" in Europe. There are many who still don't understand why you had to leave your country. They refuse to see that support isn't enough to make a life, that being isolated far from one's family is less painful than the torment of poverty and deprivation.

In Venice, I write as I walk down a long, dark, narrow corridor, trapped between the relentless image of your body and the chaotic, fleeing image of the city. Every day, these words of Proust resonate in my head: "The town that I saw before me had ceased to be Venice". Yes, this town no longer represented anything for me other than a faded postcard, with no date and no addressee.

I wrote "Alma" in my notebook. Almost automatically, as if an alien hand was guiding mine. I know nothing about her except that she's American and that she's waiting for a male friend who's supposed to be meeting her in Venice. For some unknown reason, I was naïve enough to imagine that she might be able to help me write this book, that her mere presence would give me the energy to piece together the fragments and reach a truth that had so far remained inaccessible.

The verdict was suicide. Case closed. Henceforth you would be filed away in a dusty drawer. A folder containing all the documents gathered in the course of the investigation: your train ticket and residence permit found in the plastic wallet, the receipts for the various applications you'd made since your arrival in Italy, documents from Pozzallo and Milan, the photos taken on the day you drowned, the witness statements and those from people who knew you, copies of the videos on a USB stick.

For a long time I'd been wondering what it meant to die in a city accustomed to festivals and commemorations, a city of water and light, of frescos and marble staircases, of vast ballrooms adorned with giant chandeliers and silver and gold candelabras. To die behind the scenes of a world of pomp and excess.

Alma eventually came out with the question she'd been burning to ask. She closed her book and turned her chair to face me. She looked me in the eyes and asked what I was doing in Venice. I took a deep breath and then I told her everything. I talked to her about you, about your home country, the "smiling coast of Africa", the makeshift tubs adrift, heaps of bodies, the boats that capsize, the dangerous desert crossings, men auctioned or tortured in hangars devoid of light, the torturers' unpunished evil acts, the disgraceful complicity of the powerful, the almost total silence of the world. I told her about the shattered dreams that you stowed in a backpack, the sweet memories that you abandoned on the Sicilian coast, your period of uncertainty in Pozzallo, your endless wait at Milan railway station, the train that spirited you away, the residence permit that you slipped into a plastic wallet to bequeath to the world a sign of your passing through. I told her about the invisible ogre of the Grand Canal who gobbled you up in one mouthful, about the three giant flags that continued to flutter in front of your dull gaze, about the blue body bag in which you found eternal rest, one January day in 2017.

The mayor of Venice announces that the city authorities will take care of your funeral. The press say that that will not be enough to make up either for the silence of the officials or the cries of shame on the day you drowned. The municipal gesture of respect is redolent of the unfinished. Bitterness is incurable. The tragedy leaves in its wake ripples that will not go away. Your bequest to Venice: a cracked mirror in which the entire world can see its smugness reflected.

And to think that on Ascension Day, Venetians celebrate the marriage of the city with the sea. Long ago, aboard the *Bucentaur*, the Doge would throw a gold ring into the Adriatic. Nowadays, the mayor takes part in a reconstruction of the event aboard a replica of the state barge. The former Republic of Venice wanted to trumpet its maritime supremacy and its domination of the waters. You wanted the exact opposite: to scream to the world the powerlessness of the social outcasts, the unbearable precariousness of their lives, on land and in the water. Those who set off not thinking of a return. Those for whom a real wedding is often an impossible dream. Those whose existence is trapped in a spiral of woes encircling their bodies and their memories.

At first, she listened to me religiously. She knew nothing of your story. Your name meant nothing to her either. She almost apologised, a slight tremor in her voice. She had heard of what is generally called "the tragedy of the migrants", but nothing more. She knew that people died in the Mediterranean, but she'd never burdened herself with the stories, details, and even less the names. For her, you were a plural of suffering and affliction, the collateral victims of a global imbalance. And yet, I could see she wanted to know more about you. Where you'd come from, your journey, the circumstances of your death thousands of miles from your country. Later, she would admit that she'd never heard of The Gambia and was unable to locate your country on a map. At first, I slightly held it against her.

On Friday, 27 January 2017, five days after your death,

a memorial ceremony was organised at the site of the tragedy. I found photos of it online. A crowd gathered on the steps of Santa Lucia station. Venetians rubbed shoulders with visitors. The crowd was compact. A group of fellow Africans was there. A dozen men. They had made a floral wreath in your memory.

The other night, I had a strange dream. The municipality had organised a gondola regatta to pay tribute to you. A thirty-kilometre Vogalonga in the dark. I was alone on board a gondola and I was rowing as hard as I could, but my boat wasn't moving forward. I could hear cries of distress rending the night. I felt as if the Grand Canal was going to open up and swallow me.

Alma's gaze is a bottomless well. I seek comfort, support and I don't know what else in it. I show her the file on which I've printed your name in capital letters: PATEH. She examines the photos, the articles and the press cuttings. Every so often, she pauses at a particular detail and asks me for more information. In the end, she tells me that she admires the efforts I've been making over the past few months. I don't want to reveal all to her, but I invite her to flick through my notebook. The pages flip past and it feels as if a slice of my life is gliding like a makeshift raft past the fascinated eyes of a stranger.

The wreath is in the colours of The Gambia. Red, blue and green flowers. Red for the savannah, blue for the river and green for the forests. Tied together with a white ribbon, the symbol of peace, on which your name is written. You are reunited with your home country at last. The five letters of your name at the boundary between earth and sky.

For some days in my hotel room, I've been hearing music. Someone must be playing the piano in an adjoining building. At night, I get back to work. I write with those mysterious melodies caressing the words on the page. I think about the concerts at the church of Santa Maria della Pietà, close to the former orphanage where Vivaldi taught the violin. I am reminded of Alejo Carpentier's *Baroque Concert*, a novel in which a Mexican meets Vivaldi, Handel and Domenico Scarlatti in Venice. Propelled by the music, Latin America invites itself to the banks of the Grand Canal. Words and chants mingle in a whirlwind of intoxication and magic. Then suddenly, like an epiphany, a curtain falls and your face reappears. I go back to my notebook. From the start, I've been struggling with the impossibility of writing a novel based on your story.

Alma and I talk a lot about you. She wants to get to know you, understand your situation, immerse herself in your story, put words on each stage of your journey, each wound to your body, each disappointment, each crack, each fragment released by the impact of your passage. She encouraged me to get out of the hotel finally and discover Venice. But I'd begun to appreciate my seclusion. I was afraid of giving in to the temptation of becoming a tourist. With her, something had changed. She convinced me that I had to pick up the pieces of your story wherever they were. Extend the sphere of my Venetian experience to circumscribe the void that continued to stifle your memory.

From the station esplanade, the green dome towers above the silent crowd. A few mobile phones are lit up. Some Venetians carry bouquets. Journalists wield huge cameras. Dotted among the crowd are a few Veneto regional flags. A microphone is being passed around. One speech follows another in the heavy, oppressive atmosphere. The words are slow and approximate, but the emotion is raw. And your name is spoken. A light in the winter of the lagoon. Two syllables exploding with pain and truth.

Three weeks after the tragedy, Carnival takes over the town. I wonder if people are still talking about you on that 11 February 2017, whether your shadow continues to haunt the Grand Canal. On a website, I come across a series of photos capturing the carnival-goers' excitement. As every year, the procession of long black capes, the colourful masks, the black felt tricorn hats, all those garish colours, delicate embroidery, those undulating forms, quivering feathers, and concealed faces. Shielded by the secrecy of the Carnival, their anonymity has nothing in common with yours. I have the sense that less than one month after your death, Venice has become the dark stage of a theatre where bodies have been replaced by shadows and where the riot of colours has no equivalent but the cloak of silence that has enveloped your name.

Aboard a Line 2 vaporetto, I experience for the first time a sense of relief. The silhouette of the station recedes and it is as if a door were closing slowly behind your story. Beside me, Alma is pensive. I wonder whether she's had the time to digest everything that I've told her about you. As we go beyond the Bridge of the Barefoot Monks, I have the feeling that eyes hidden in the shadows continue to watch the spot from which you jumped. In the past few days, my hallucinations have taken a disquieting turn. I refrain from telling Alma about them. I don't want to worry her. The buildings on either side of the Grand Canal look shrunken, diminished, as if crushed by the hand of an invisible giant.

A man steps forward holding a floral wreath aloft, like an offering to the heavens. He's wearing a scarf with "Venezia" printed on it. A continent flows in his veins, outlines on his face a faint, unexpected, almost miraculous smile. Behind him, the other faces are grim. Beanie hats pulled down over their dejected heads. To the left, a photographer is adjusting the settings on his camera. All eyes are on the flowers.

On reading an article about cats in Venice, I think of those boats in the seventeenth century bringing back from Syria the combative cat breed that would exterminate the rats. The plague had ravaged the town and now an Asian bloodline would land on the Venetian shores as a saviour. These days, alley cats are scarce. The city authorities no longer appreciate them because they are a nuisance to tourists. Strange fate, that of those prized felines, revered and then abandoned. But here and there, animal rights associations campaign to protect Venice's cats. Humans' short memories will never get the better of their emotions.

Beneath the arcades of the Rialto market, I notice shapes advancing slowly, as in a strange procession. A few metres further on, the vaporetto stops and I signal to Alma that we should get off. The arch of the Rialto bridge is a smile hanging in the sky.

When the man with the "Venezia" scarf throws the wreath into the water, a slight shiver ripples through the crowd. As if they were reliving one last time the exact moment when you jumped into the Grand Canal. As if your entire story were there, condensed into those flowers already drifting away, carrying with them the colours of your country and the echo of your name.

And the city with its procession of masked criminals, thieves, some of them violent, evil swindlers, unscrupulous men capable of every type of scam, every type of offence. Suddenly, the thought of your death was simply engulfed, obliterated by those that had preceded it. That entire Venetian imaginary of death which ended up prevailing, normalising the macabre and indirectly effacing the traces of your passage.

We have just turned into Calle Bembo when Alma slips her hand into mine. I don't know where we're going, but I still have that same feeling of wellbeing. The street is narrow and we walk past several tourists standing in front of the restaurant doors or window-gazing. Neither the damaged gutters nor the faded façades dampen my mood. We come out onto Calle del Teatro o della Comedia and I'm glad to be back in the daylight. An elderly couple are arguing outside a clothes shop. Three young people sitting on some steps are sharing a pizza, laughing. A little farther away, three flags are fluttering on the frontage of the Goldoni theatre. I'm reminded of the façade of the Hotel Carlton and the shouts echoing from one side of the Grand Canal to the other. A yellow sign points the way to St Mark's Square.

Beneath Venice, your name is lost in an invisible forest of oaks and larches. Erosion is relentless, despite the Istrian stone imported from the Balkans. In the town as in your story, there's something that's persistently crumbling. A dislocation process that nothing seems capable of halting.

The floral wreath makes a dull splash as it drops into the water. Then applause breaks out. Four or five flowers immediately come adrift. But your name is still there, intact on the white ribbon. Cradled by the water, the wreath slowly floats away. Pateh, here you are sailing on the Grand Canal like a pirogue setting off towards the land of your ancestors.

I squeeze Alma's hand a little harder and we head down Calle dei Fabbri. I look up and see hundreds of half-open shutters. We pass an illegal hawker carrying a dozen fake designer handbags. There's a sad look in his eyes, an indescribable hint of nostalgia. I'd read that many Senegalese try to earn a living that way in Venice and elsewhere in Italy. They're often hounded by the police. They endure abuse and are always ready to run off. The man darts us a furtive glance then vanishes into the next street.

How many foreigners have ended up in the water in Venice? How many have died and how many managed to survive? I read somewhere that in 1819, Lord Byron slipped as he was stepping into a gondola. And yet he was a frequent visitor to Venice. He was easily able to swim in the Grand Canal. Apparently, he would often swim back to the Palazzo Mocenigo where he was staying.

In the photo, a dozen hands pressed together in prayer beside the water. Brothers who'd arrived in Venice well before you. Supposing you had run into one of them on the day you arrived? He might have offered you accommodation, or made suggestions about your options, helped you to change your plans or find temporary work. But on that January day in 2017, outside the station there was no one to welcome you.

I shan't talk about the monuments or the souvenir shops, even less about the tourists with their raucous laughter, sophisticated cameras and their maps unfurled haphazardly. All I retain from that stroll with Alma is the softness of her hand in mine and the tremors that ran through my body each time she squeezed it a little harder. I couldn't say whether we were starting to have feelings for each other, but I do have one certainty: something in your story is bringing us together, a sort of secret pact that would not exist without you. In the darkness of the Sotoportego dei Dai, I want to stop and question Alma. Ask her for news of her friend and why she decided to follow a stranger obsessed with the story of a dead man.

Freeze frame on that collective prayer at the spot where you drowned. Palms outspread, bodies pressed together, heads slightly bowed. Your soul is there, under the collective gaze of those men who are reliving their own disjointed stories, their chaotic arrival on the shores of Europe, the succession of brutalities and humiliations they have suffered, their shared fear of losing everything, of being sent back and having to start all over again. Your name is on all the lips that are murmuring words of compassion, calling for God's clemency and mercy, dreaming in silence of a new day on the lagoon.

Each photo of the ceremony on the station esplanade

carries the promise of a story to come. One of them shows a man photographed from behind. He's wearing a grey hat and a blue jacket, and his arms are folded. His gaze is fixed on the wreath drifting away from the shore. It is like a farewell scene revisited by a contemporary painter.

Apparently, there was a time when a Venetian newspaper published a daily list of people who had fallen into the water and, according to the legend, any foreigner who had that disagreeable experience, was baptised a Venetian, as if following a secret ritual of the city. It suddenly dawned on me: you died a Venetian, Pateh! From the moment your body touched the water, this town became yours. For barely a few minutes.

Arriving at St Mark's Square, we stop in our tracks. At first, I can't believe my eyes. The square is deserted. Completely deserted. Not a soul. Initially, I think it's yet another hallucination, but I read the same astonishment on Alma's face. The campanile is a solitary arrow touching the heavens. The basilica looks like a huge toy, almost unreal, its façade resembling a "cardboard cutout music-hall frontage" as described by Maupassant. The feeling that everything could crumble as in a dream with fragile, uncertain boundaries.

How long did the wreath float on the water? Little does it matter because it too vanished. Like you. Like your body and your memory.

With you, I learned to push writing to its limits, in other words resist the temptation to interpret, to rip off the masks to reveal the spaces and concertina time. The aim of each fragment is to oppose hollow speeches with the energy of evocation. I never wanted to go to Venice. Perhaps I wasn't able to be there fully. But walking in your footsteps, I put my own limits to the test.

In the middle of St Mark's Square, time seems to be standing still. I wonder what Alma and I are doing here, facing the remnants of the Republic of Venice. Everything is as if the square were going to close over us, as if the arcades were going to collapse and leave a vast field of ruins. Alma's arms are trembling. She snuggles up to me and, for the first time, I can feel her heart beating against mine. With one accord, we decide to walk in the direction of the Grand Canal. In the distance, a light appears between two columns.

Later, I read that the men who took part in the ceremony had nearly all come from reception centres in the Mestre district. The demonstration, called "A wreath for Pateh" had been organised by the association La Casa di Amadou, a meeting place for asylum seekers and refugees founded by Father Don Nandino Capovilla from the Marghera parish.

On 30 August 2017, in other words, seven months after the tragedy, the Venice International Film Festival opened at the Lido. You probably saw the poster at the

Ferrovia stop, a stone's throw from the spot where you jumped. I learn that that year the film that won the Golden Lion was Guillermo del Toro's *The Shape of Water*. It takes place in a high-security US government laboratory where a mute woman cleaner discovers a mysterious scaled creature from South America that lives in a water tank. The title refers to Plato's theory that in its purest form, water takes the shape of an icosahedron, a twenty-sided polyhedron, invoking the idea that humanity has many faces. The irreducible difference of our lives. The raison d'être for my fragmented writing.

At the foot of the column supporting the winged lion, there's an elderly man seated at what looks like an easel. At his feet is an open box containing paints and brushes. When we reach him, we see that he has his head in his hands and appears to be dozing. The canvas on the easel is blank, untouched.

On the station esplanade, after the speeches and the applause, there is a sense of duty accomplished. Men and women stand in silent reflection. Others stop by the water's edge and close their eyes. Your presence is somehow a link, a promise of a better future.

What would a film telling your story be like? I picture a camera going back and forth between Banjul and Venice, filming the two towns simultaneously, avoiding both shortcuts and commonplaces. A rebel camera that would resist tourist voyeurism and vulgar exoticism. A sensitive camera that would reveal the spirit of your homeland and the uncertainty of the countries you passed through. A camera that would join the dots between all the places where you dragged your wretchedness the way a raincloud about to burst drags across the sky.

The old man looks up and we see a face furrowed by age. His eyes light up. He strokes his white beard and, with a slight nod, invites us to sit down on the two stools that he produces out of nowhere, like a magician. I have no wish to leave with a portrait, but a glint in Alma's eye convinces me otherwise. We sit down on the stools. The old man adjusts the canvas on the easel.

Several newspaper articles quote this declaration by the head of the Mestre branch of the Italian lifeguards association: "[…] but maybe something more could have been done to save him." It is clear that that "more" would have required an additional effort, a presence of mind, a clear-headedness that no one had. In the photos of the homage paid to you, there is a shadow of remorse and regret. A shadow that hangs over the station esplanade, envelops the floral wreath and sows thorns in the hearts of the locals and the foreigners. Would words be enough to chase away that pernicious shadow?

In novel after novel, the inert body of Venice spreads endlessly. The city of the dead shaped by the imaginations of writers of every ilk, starting with the bards of Romanticism and Decadence. I write as I battle against the city's morbid memory.

His movements are slow, but his brushstrokes are particularly intense. Who is this old man? A famous painter fallen on hard times or an impoverished amateur who makes a living painting portraits of tourists? Alma sits stock still on the stool. I take advantage of a moment when the painter's attention is glued to his canvas to glance at her. For the first time, I find her beauty perfect. My gaze follows the line of her neck, the outline of her lips, the shape of her eyebrows and her eyes. Alma, like a mirage in flesh and blood bound up with the city of the dead.

Gradually, the witness statements confirm the sickness you suffered from. They speak of a profound ill which apparently began to gnaw at you from your arrival in Italy. I wonder whether it doesn't date from earlier. Like an invasive plant whose branches grew slowly deep inside you. A venomous plant that fed on your breath, your memory, your fear of failure so close to your goal, on your being the target of accusatory or contemptuous looks. A plant that the famous "immigration policies" nurtured with clichés and stereotypes. A plant that you wished you could uproot so as to be able to breathe deeply at last.

Each time I try to put my notes in order, I come up against this fact: there is perhaps no form of writing that can "accommodate" your tragedy. Neither fiction nor narrative. Neither imaginary confession nor poetic or fictionalised biography. This requiem is like the lagoon: parcels of land surrounded by water and uncertainty. A cloud of dust, a procession of fragments, pieces that nothing can bring together other than the persistent taste of defeat.

The scratching of the paintbrush on the surface of the canvas. The creaking of the easel. The old man's ponderous silence. Everything seems to be enfolding us, bringing us close, almost making us forget the empty square. Are we really in Venice or are we in an invisible town, created by centuries of myths and fantasies?

Every week, the parish of Marghera opens its doors to refugees and asylum-seekers. Among them are many of your fellow citizens. Gambians a long way from their country, united by your memory. For Father Don Nandino Capovilla, it is pointless to continue the discussion about how you should have been rescued. The most important thing is to rethink the reception of refugees, to open people's arms and eyes to "what is coming".

"Disgrace." The word falls onto the page like a shell. I discard the shrapnel so as to gauge the weight of those eight incisive letters.

Now, the old man is glancing furtively at us, as if he wanted to check that we hadn't got up from our stools. The lampposts dotted around the column are like those on the station esplanade. Solitary and widely spaced, like strange silhouettes of sleepwalkers about to jump into the Grand Canal. A stray pigeon lands close to the easel as if it were a sign reminding us that there was something extraordinary about this moment.

According to the Italian press, your cousin staying at the Frosinone reception centre seventy kilometres south-east of Rome launched a crowdfunder to help the family to repatriate your body. He also thanked all those who attended the memorial ceremony. Your family heard about this solidarity campaign.

I write between tragedy and remembrance, in the interstices where the shards of your memory reappear.

What is a work of art if not the mystery of an appearance, the blast of an explosion that the hand cannot grasp, that the eye tries to follow with a mixture of anguish and satisfaction? I am haunted by the question during the endless minutes facing the old man who seems to be putting the final touches to the painting. Alma has just rested her head on my right shoulder. I don't realise at first that she is silently crying.

Venetian photographers from the Awakening collective produced a poster in your memory. It shows the gathering that took place on the station esplanade. It shows the men praying in a circle after throwing the wreath into the Grand Canal. But the poster did not survive the return of hatred. Barely pasted up, contemptuous hands tore it into shreds and threw it into the bin. I read about the photographers' fury. They call it "an action in poor taste". We live in an era where fraternity is garbage, a suspicious and undesirable motive.

When I leave Venice, I will go and honour your memory on the station esplanade. I'll take my notebook and read you a few excerpts from my writing facing the Grand Canal, the exact spot where the wreath bore away your name.

Absorbed in drying the tears running down Alma's cheeks, I do not notice that the old man has risen to study his canvas. A smile of contentment finally appears on his face. He takes a few steps back and cocks his head to the left and then to the right, as if to check that all the details have been executed perfectly. His hands in his pockets, he looks up at the winged lion and mutters a few words; it takes me a while to realise that he's praying.

A year later, the crowd gathers once more to renew its tribute. The faces are less tense. Time has done its work, made furrows in the friable stuff of memory. People sing and pray for your memory to remain a beacon through the years. Another wreath is thrown into the Grand Canal. Each year, the colours of your country will be reborn in Venetians' hearts.

To say that this city has helped me to write this book

would be to exaggerate its role. All I know is that I have learned as much about Venice as about you. I have occupied that liminal space between two lagoons, two geographies attached to your name.

When the old man takes down the painting and invites us to take a few steps towards the Grand Canal, I am a little surprised, but Alma beckons me to follow him. He walks ahead of us. We can see only the back of the canvas. Behind us, a sudden army of pigeons invades St Mark's Square.

I wonder whether the crowd will come back this year to pay tribute to your memory, whether the refugees and the new arrivals will renew their collective prayer, whether the white ribbon emblazoned with your name will stay tied around the flowers, as if to ward off for ever the shadow of oblivion.

It is decided, I'll leave Venice and go to Banjul. I'll go and seek other traces in your home country. I've checked the flights. I'll stop over in Lisbon. I'll go alone and find a way of disappearing. Alma shouldn't have to suffer my quest or follow my wanderings. She should meet up with her friend and enjoy her holiday. Your story is a wound that I carry deep within me, fragments of which will continue to haunt me for months and perhaps years. I know that there will always be something of you in my future writings, in my unfinished projects and my temporary drafts.

Facing the Grand Canal, the old man turns around and we brace ourselves to see our portraits. I can barely conceal a slight excitement. Alma hugs me a little tighter.

I've left some blank pages in my notebook. There's no point telling all, explaining everything. Allow silence or others the opportunity to say the rest.

Before leaving Venice, I'll write Alma a letter. I'll find the words to tell her of the joy of our encounter and the bond we forged over your memory. I'll tell her about my book, about this unfinished requiem that has obsessed me for a long time and that I must now extricate from this city and share with the world. On the day of my departure, I'll leave the letter and a copy of my notebook at the hotel reception desk.

And the canvas is unveiled before our astonished eyes. We are not in it. Neither my face nor Alma's, but yours. Yes, Pateh, I see your portrait. I immediately recognise your eyes, your thin moustache, your black jacket. Around you, men and women are sitting in a circle, their hands joined in a collective prayer. On your head is that same wreath that was thrown into the Grand Canal the other day. I recognise the colours of your country and the white ribbon emblazoned with your name in capital letters.

REFERENCES

Epigraph, Aimé Césaire, "The Automatic Crystal" in Aimé Césaire, *The Collected Poetry,* translated by Clayton Eshleman and Annette Smith, Los Angeles/London, University of Berkeley Press, 1983.

p. 4. *Return to my Native Land*, Aimé Césaire, translated by John Berger and Anna Bostock, Penguin Modern Classics, 2024.

p. 8. Title translates as "In the country of the disappeared". Not available in English.

p. 19. Carlo Goldoni, *Memoirs of Carlo Goldoni*, translated by John Black, Boston, Osgood, 1877.

p. 23. Michel Tournier, *Les Météores*, Gallimard, 1975; English title *Gemini*, trans. Anne Carter, Collins, 1981.

p. 27. Thomas Mann, *Death in Venice*, translated by Kenneth Burke, New York, Alfred A. Knopf, 1925.

p. 29. Limojon de Saint-Didier, *La Ville et la République de Venise,* Amsterdam, Daniel Elsevier, 1680. Not translated into English.

p. 33. Marc Alyn, *Venise, démons et merveilles,* Éditions Ecriture, 2014. Not translated into English.

p. 37. Philippe Sollers, *Éloge de l'infini*, Gallimard, 2002. Not translated into English.

p. 94. Ernest Hemingway, *Across the River and Into the Trees*, New York, Charles Scribner's Sons, 1950.

p. 97. Marcel Proust, *Albertine disparue*, the sixth volume of *À la recherche du temps perdu*. It was translated by Terence Kilmartin as *Albertine Gone,* London: Chatto & Windus, 1989.

p. 109. Guy de Maupassant, *La Vie errante*, 1890.

ABOUT THE AUTHOR AND TRANSLATOR

Khalid Lyamlahy, born in Rabat, Morocco in 1986, is an Assistant Professor of French and Francophone Studies at the University of Chicago, where he teaches North African literature. He completed a PhD in Francophone Studies at Oxford, and is the author of *Nostalgic Rebels: Politics, Aesthetics, and Selfhood in Postcolonial Morocco* (Liverpool University Press, 2025). His first novel, *Un roman étranger*, was published in 2017. This second novel, published in French as *Évocation d'un mémorial à Venise* in 2023, was shortlisted for the Prix Alain Spiess in 2023. In 2024 it won the Prix Éthiophile and was awarded the Special Mention of the Prix des Cinq Continents.

Ros Schwartz is an award-winning translator from French. Acclaimed for her new version of Antoine de Saint-Exupéry's *The Little Prince* (published in 2010), she has over 100 fiction and nonfiction titles to her name. She is one of the team retranslating George Simenon's novels for Penguin Classics. She has translated a number of Francophone writers including Tahar ben Jelloun, Fatou Diome and Ousmane Sembène and most recently Max Lobe's *A Long Way from Douala* (HopeRoad) and *Does Snow Turn a Person White Inside*, by the same author.

ABOUT HOPEROAD AND SMALL AXES

Founded in 2010, HopeRoad's mission has been to promote literary voices from Africa, Asia and the Caribbean. The name comes from a road in Jamaica where Bob Marley lived and which is now home to the Bob Marley Museum at 56 Hope Road. In exploring themes of identity, cultural stereotyping and disability, we bring neglected voices from the margins to the centre of the page in a range of books for adults and young adults.

Started in 2019, Small Axes takes its name from the Bob Marley song, "Small Axe": a well sharp axe ready to cut the big tree down. The imprint mixes postcolonial classics with titles by contemporary authors that continue in the tradition of rebellion and contesting the canon. Successes include *Inspector Dreadlock Holmes* by John Agard; *A Long Way from Douala* by Max Lobe; *The Black and White Museum* by Ferdinand Dennis; *The Last One* by Fatima Daas and *The Nowhere Man* and *Nectar in a Sieve* by Kamala Markandaya.

Since February 2024, the physical production, marketing and publicity for HopeRoad titles has been handled by Peepal Tree Press. We are very happy to be joining forces with a fellow independent with a compatible ethos and complementary publishing identity.

We hope that the books we publish not only give pleasure and joy but that they also help to open minds and attitudes to diversity. We are pleased to be publishing in a period of cultural flux when more and more voices from outside the mainstream are being heard.

If you would like to support our work, please stay in touch online and via social media, details below.

Rosemarie Hudson, Publisher and Founder of HopeRoad
Pete Ayrton, Editor Small Axes

hoperoadpublishing.com | @hoperoadpublish